a Ross

BRIGHTON ROCK

Notes on English Literature

CHIEF ADVISER: John D. Jump
Professor of English Literature in the University of Manchester

GENERAL EDITOR: W. H. Mason
Sometime Senior English Master Manchester Grammar School

BRIGHTON ROCK

(GRAHAM GREENE)

A. PRICE

Senior Lecturer in Education
Queen's University, Belfast

BASIL BLACKWELL
OXFORD

PRINTED IN GREAT BRITAIN
BY LONSDALE & BARTHOLOMEW (LEICESTER) LTD
AND BOUND BY KEMP HALL BINDERY, OXFORD

CONTENTS

GENERAL NOTE

This series of introductions to the great classics of English literature is designed primarily for the school, college, and university student, although it is hoped that they will be found helpful by a much larger audience. Three aims have been kept in mind:

(A) To give the reader the relevant information necessary for his fuller understanding of the work.

(B) To indicate the main areas of critical interest, to suggest suitable critical approaches, and to point out possible critical difficulties.

(C) To do this in as simple and lucid a manner as possible, avoiding technical jargon and giving a full explanation of any critical terms employed.

Each introduction contains questions on the text and suggestions for further reading. It should be emphasized that in no sense is any introduction to be considered as a substitute for the reader's own study, understanding, and appreciation of the work.

The figures following quotations show their source; e.g. (5, vi) refers to Part Five, section six.

THE COMPREHENSIVENESS
OF BRIGHTON ROCK

In his novels Graham Greene combines the topical and the universal.

A scarlet racing model, a tiny rakish car which carried about it the atmosphere of innumerable road-houses, of totsies gathered round swimming pools, of furtive encounters in by-lanes off the Great North Road, wormed through the traffic with incredible dexterity. (4, i).

This is contemporary—in the items, the slang and the skill in manipulating machines it indicates, and also in the atmosphere of flashy, rootless sophistication. Yet the appetites and moral issues involved are common to every age.

Something similar applies, with deeper and more diverse implications, to the following passage.

A mounted policeman came up the road: the lovely cared-for chestnut beast stepping delicately on the hot macadam, like an expensive toy a millionaire buys for his children; you admired the finish, the leather as deeply glowing as an old mahogany table top, the bright silver badge; it never occurred to you that the toy was for use. It never occurred to Hale, watching the policeman pass; he couldn't appeal to him. A man stood by the kerb selling objects on a tray; he had lost the whole of one side of the body: leg and arm and shoulder; and the beautiful horse as it paced by turned its head aside delicately like a dowager. 'Shoelaces,' the man said hopelessly to

Hale, 'matches.' Hale didn't hear him. 'Razor blades.' Hale went by, the words lodged securely in his brain: the thought of the thin wound and the sharpness of the agony. That was how Kite was killed. (i, i).

Here a flavour of the nineteen-thirties is conveyed, through the objects—'hot macadam', 'shoelaces' and 'matches', the social gulf between the maimed ex-serviceman and the dowager (further suggested by the difference between the hideous, neglected man and the lovely cared-for beast), and the policeman, seeming so free and powerful, yet really a thing in the hands of those who use him to maintain the social order. There is no help for the maimed man, nor for Hale (mentally maimed) since he has put himself on the wrong side of the law by being involved in the murder of Kite, which is recalled and Hale's impending doom shown most sharply by 'razor blades'. All this is modern, the stuff of the popular press, and the commercialized mass media, the world of Hitchcock and the crime-thriller. But at the same time the elements involved—the callousness of the rich towards the poor, the majesty and glitter of the law covering its brute strength and remorseless pro-cesses (often influenced by political factors), the guilt of the creature fleeing from vengeance and, because he has not expiated his crime, precluded from an appeal to justice (Divine Mercy he ignores) and liable to sense the horror of retribution in an innocent expression—all these elements occur in nearly every generation and race. It all adds up to the profound suggestion that although Brighton, our urban existence, is like this, vain, unjust and corrupted, the world essentially, however different its guises, has always been the same; as Drewitt puts it, drawing on Marlowe and a sombre and powerful tradition: 'this is Hell, nor are we out of it.' (7, iii). In Newman's words: 'the human race is implicated in some terrible aboriginal calamity.' To Greene also 'human nature is not black and white but black and grey', and this belief is central in *Brighton Rock*.

Though there is a lot more to be said about this and about the other considerations just touched on and the fusing of topicality and universality, it is apparent how much Greene succinctly comprehends, what peculiar riches in a little room he provides. His grasp of the shifting manifestations, the textures, the sense impressions of the everyday world, and his awareness of the enduring social, mental and spiritual forces permeating it, are clear throughout *Brighton Rock* and may be well exemplified by the first section of Part Four.

This echoes the opening of the novel. There is a similar exuberance and hard-won pleasure in the air, and there is also pursuit and betrayal and violence. But in Part Four the gaiety of the crowd is shot through with seriousness; they don't spend their money, they harbour it; there are bets to be laid, much to be won or lost, hopes to be fulfilled or plans to go wrong, issues to be decided by skill or deception or fortune. All press absorbed in one direction, to the races; individuals surging intent with a single desire, 'like some natural and irrational migration of insects'; crammed vehicles so thick that the whole road seems to move 'upwards like an underground staircase' and suggests (in view of what Brighton seems to represent) various levels or stages in Hades. Outside this turbulent flow and in telling contrast to it, stand three groups: the Negro ('Black Boy' wins the race) sits alone and content, proud of the cigar between his 'cushiony lips', his manner and words simple and unformed like those of the children, interested but uneasy, being unused to coloured people (this places the scene in the 1930's rather than in the 1960's); then the blind band, driven into the gutter, able to move only by feeling the kerb, their attempts at putting on a brave show (blinded pit ponies trying to be tigers) only making more palpable and pathetic their pain and dereliction; and finally the daughters of the rich on their aristocratic turf, protected and aloof from the plebeian procession and turf, the senior girls feeling the unusual excitement but repressing it completely and solemnly concentrating on the higher rites of hockey, the juniors not yet so well trained taking to their heels like ponies racing natural and carefree (unlike the blinded pit ponies or the horses racing for money).

The items which make up this moving picture are seen from a distance, a panorama over which the eye goes perceptively. Then we move nearer to the scarlet racing car and the woman singing "something traditional about brides and bouquets, something which went with stout and oysters", and we recall Ida and her journey in the taxi with the doomed Hale and the old Morris car in pursuit. And then we see the Morris again and its occupants but this time they are apprehensive and divided and one intends to kill the other.

This treachery of Pinkie's gives irony to his remarks to Spicer about arranging a lasting peace, 'Have a good time while you're here', 'I won't be seeing you again', 'Well, this is good-bye'—and to Spicer's backing of Memento Mori and his cry to the bookmaker (as Colleoni's men are about to attack), 'now the pay-off'. But it is Pinkie who gets the biggest shock. Life seems good, he is in his element on the race-course, toying sadistically with Spicer; then it all turns on him: 'Pain happened to him; and he was filled with horror and astonishment as if one of the bullied brats at school had stabbed first with the dividers'; the mob enjoyed themselves carving him, 'just as he had always enjoyed himself,' and he wept with pain and humiliation.

There is a further shocking revelation: he can't repent. He has always comforted himself that no matter what he did he could always escape punishment by repenting at the last moment: 'Between the stirrup and the ground, he mercy sought and mercy found'. (3, iii). But, as Rose feared, he does not have time or energy, his habits hold him and he is out of the way of prayer, 'and he remembered Kite, after they'd got him at St. Pancras, passing out in the waiting-room, while a porter poured coal dust on the dead grate, talking all the time about someone's tits'. (4, i). Dying, Kite was typically gross, and this is how it is, in a crisis your whole personality reacts as it has been set, at a level far deeper than the conscious or rational. You behave as you have been accustomed to behave and you cannot suddenly switch to an opposite stance or manner; only those used to praying and confessing can pray and confess in extremity. This important truth, Pinkie, as he cowers, hurt and humiliated, in the drab garage possessed with squalid images, seems about to notice; perhaps in this darkness he should begin to make his peace. But the notion, selfish and conceited, that he has had Spicer eliminated, braces him, and although 'his heart weakened with a faint nostalgia for the tiny dark confessional box, the priest's voice and the people waiting under the statue', his pride, his besetting sin, pushes the truth aside. Sadistically he crushes a wounded moth (perhaps an image of his faint nostalgia for the church), and then, his self-esteem growing with his self-dramatizing, he limps back, a young dictator, after only a temporary defeat, still confident that he can avoid divine retribution by trickery or bribes. The contrast between his unbounded spiritual pride and his feeble physical condition is marked by the passing of Colleoni and a smart woman in a luxurious car. Pinkie has not been able to outwit Colleoni, but he continues to be certain that he will be too much for God.

Rose possesses the spiritual strength he lacks, but it is only for physical rehabilitation that he goes to her. She does not fail. Yet, ironically, her distress, her identification of herself with him and her anger and scorn against Ida and the rest increase his pride. And also ironically her devotion—'Pinkie, I love you. . . I don't care what you've done . . . I'd rather burn with you than be like Her'—is characteristically misunderstood by him. He cannot see that her vow means simply that she will always be true to him, whatever happens, that there is no need to do anything further to bind her to him. He 'had to have peace'; and she offers it him absolutely. But this kind of truth is beyond his ken. Calculating to be safe from the law by means of the law, he seeks, while shuddering with loathing, to marry her, not realizing that her love infinitely more than any legal bond would prevent her from letting him down. Thus he involves himself in wearying schemes which turn out to be vain, for there is never scope for making them sound, there is only bare expediency: 'Life was a series of complicated tactical exercises, as complicated as the alignments at Waterloo, thought out on a brass bedstead among the crumbs of sausage roll. . . . The Boy pulled her up to him; tactics, tactics: there was never any time for strategy; and in the grey night light he could see her face lifted for a kiss. He wanted to strike her, to make her scream, but he kissed her inexpertly'.

This vain activity is brought home palpably when he returns anxiously to Billy's. After declaring that Spicer is dead, Pinkie is shocked to come across him hastily packing and aware that his life is sought. To murder Spicer, to marry Rose, entails further complications and expense; Drewitt must be involved, the risks are materially increased. For Pinkie, things are bad—so different from the outlook of a few hours previously when life seemed good in the sunshine on the race-course walking 'towards the finest of all sensations, the infliction of pain'. His case perhaps is similar to that of Macbeth on the appearance of Banquo's ghost; and so is his response—to go on killing, being 'in blood stepped in so far that, should [he] wade no more, Returning were as tedious as go o'er'. The ghost, however, that has plagued Pinkie most resolutely throughout this momentous chapter and done him harm likely to prove fatal (like the ghost of Caesar plaguing his murderers at Philippi) is the ghost of Fred Hale.

After the cremation Ida had tried to get in touch with Fred's spirit by means of the shifty Old Crowe and 'The Board'. As is often the case, the oracle's pronouncement was interpreted by the petitioner according to her own needs and satisfaction. She felt that she was divinely ordained to avenge Fred, to make his murderers 'sorry they was ever born'. (i, iii). It was going to be exciting, fun, a bit of life. But to accomplish her mission she has to have money, so she backs Fred's tip, Black Boy.

Hence throughout the race-course scene, Fred's presence is felt decisively, and Pinkie senses 'an invisible power working against him'. This power, after being foreshadowed perhaps in the enigmatic negro, confident and prosperous, who appears in the first paragraph of the section, operates through Ida. She is never seen by Pinkie but he continually hears her or hears of her. Her carefree, ripe Guinness voice blows back upon Pinkie and Spicer; her songs about marriage (which he hates and fears) sting Pinkie, and the final word of one of them, 'wreath', drifts ominously across Pinkie's double-edged remark that no one is going to break the peace he is arranging. Spicer reports that a woman has backed Black Boy to win two hundred and fifty pounds. Pinkie flatly declares that Black Boy won't win, adding, with tremendous unconscious irony, that if he did want to celebrate, 'it wouldn't be with Black Boy'. He is much more correct here than he realizes, just as his following remarks that he 'wouldn't call that a lucky horse ... Fred never knew a good horse from a bad one. That crazy polony's dropped a pony. It's not *her* lucky day' prove to be fatally incorrect. Spicer's cry, 'And she's won too ... What a break! Now what about Black Boy?' means that Pinkie has lost—in a disastrous way he never imagines. Anxiety burns in him and he thinks if he were not above

it he would be scared that 'Fred's horse' had won,
and just then as if to feed his fear he hears 'a laugh, a
female laugh, mellow and confident'. It is Ida, it is
the ghost of Fred through the medium of Ida, rejoicing
at the victory. The heat is now on Pinkie. Ida, her
sinews of war well supplied, will be remorselessly on
his trail. Pinkie, of course, does not understand all
this, but he is uneasy. To restore himself he characteristically draws on his pride (scorning superstition) and
seeks to hurt, turning on Spicer 'with secret venom,
cruelty straightening his body like lust', and leading
him to the pay-off. But Pinkie also is double-crossed,
and again the mocking spirit of Fred is sensed in the
recollection of Colleoni's laughter on the telephone and
in the grins of his men as they have their fun, carving
Pinkie and shooing him away like a cat. And the
mockery persists, for a little later on, as Pinkie is
telling Rose that Spicer is dead, 'a loud laugh came
down the passage from the restaurant, a woman's
laugh, full of beer and good fellowship and no regrets.
"*She's* back," the Boy said.'

The leading importance of this first section, Part
Four, in the structure of the novel is marked. Through
it the dead man acts, Ida obtains the money without
which she would have been powerless ('That horse has
got to win ... I can't hold out else' she had said
earlier); Fred's word is shown to be true; and Ida
receiving the winnings from his tip as a sure sign from
beyond the grave that vengeance is hers goes into
action, her breasts buoyant, like 'a warship on the right
side in a war to end wars' (4, ii). Through this section
Pinkie is severely hit; he is tricked and has to face an
armed foe for the first time and knows pain and

indignity; his comfort that he can cheat punishment by repenting finally is shown to be false, and the whole-hearted love of Rose and the revival of Spicer drive him into even trickier schemes.

The section is also notable for displaying some of the chief characteristics of the novel. First, there is the use of crime-thriller devices and situations—surging, mechanized urban life, the crowds and contrasts and traffic, the tight-lipped, somewhat conventional dialogue and jargon (often loaded with irony and ambiguity as in the exchanges between Spicer and Pinkie), the frame-up, the double-cross, the gang fight, the appearance of the police, the chase, the tawdry refuge, the wounded man dragging himself to his girl-friend for help, the persistence of the private crime investigator, and the shock of the re-appearance of the gang member betrayed and supposedly dead. Connected with these are various cinematic techniques of long-shot, middle-distance shot, close-up, panning, zooming in, tracking, cross-cutting and dissolving—all apparent in the first three or four pages of the section. The eyes—all senses in fact—are constantly appealed to by the spare, vivid writing ('the horses went by, their hoofs padding like boxing-gloves on the turf'). The routine heartless cheer of Ida, her candy-floss hilarity, is caught exactly by this: 'One had heard that laugh in a hundred places: dry-eyed, uncaring, looking on the bright side, when the boats drew out and other people wept; saluting the bawdy joke in music halls; beside sick beds and in crowded Southern Railway compartments; when the wrong horse won, a good sports-woman's laugh'. And caught too is the tainted gentility, the fake poise and suavity of Drewitt: 'He came into the room with hollow joviality, a dockside manner; he had long pointed polished shoes which caught the light. Everything about him, from his breeziness to his morning coat was brand-new, except himself, and that had aged in many law courts, with many victories more damaging than defeats . . . his striped trousers were like a wedding guest's, hired for the day at Moss's; when he crossed the room, yellowly smiling, he might have been about to kiss the bride'. Glancing social comments are made, the contrast between the blind band and the daughters of the rich, between the aristocratic turf and the trampled turf of the race-course. And some of the dislikes of the author are revealed incidentally: a bookmaker has 'a smug smiling nonconformist face'; the tic-tac man makes masonic passes, and Colleoni's men have grinning Semitic faces. There is always the striking aptness of the images, such as that following Cubitt's bellow of laughter (which further sours Pinkie against him) after Pinkie says he is getting married: 'Behind his head the blind was half drawn down, shutting out the night sky, leaving the chimney-pots, black and phallic, palely smoking up into the moonlit air'. This, maybe, foreshadows the wicked ('black') sexual act for which Pinkie has no relish ('palely') which ends his virginity and invades Rose's innocence and maidenhood (of which the moon is an emblem) while the smoke, maybe, represents, in Rose's case, the incense, climbing to God, of a sacrifice for good and of thanksgiving for a child conceived, and, in Pinkie's case, the burning vapours of the flung vitriol of his final plunge into perdition. This is perhaps attaching too much significance to one expression, but there is no doubt about the way in which Greene can build singular meaning into an ordinary phrase by repeating it in certain contexts; for instance, in the use of 'the game'. Cubitt lewdly throws out the phrase, and Pinkie ponders on it. For him it is merely a notion not a real experience (to use Newman's vital distinction between a notional assent and a real assent); Pinkie 'knew the moves, he'd never played the game'. And he studies Drewitt, trying to learn the secrets, for Drewitt had been 'Twenty-five years at the game'. This expression focuses Pinkie's perverse and pervasive horror of sex: 'He didn't want *that* relationship with anyone: the double bed, the intimacy, it sickened him like the idea of age. . . To marry—it was like ordure on the hands'. The sight of two lovers 'pricked him with nausea and cruelty. He limped by them, his cut hand close on the blade'. (The open razor is a phallic symbol—he much prefers to cherish and use that rather than his own natural male organ.) He limped by 'with his cruel virginity, which demanded some satisfaction different from theirs, habitual, brutish, and short'. This sadism reaches a peak charged with a distasteful sexual impulse as Pinkie watches with rising excitement and cruelty the long strip of sticking-plaster lining Spicer's cheek and lusts 'to tear it away and see the skin break'.

Twisted or tainted energies, seediness, human absurdities and evasions occur everywhere: 'A hatless tout delayed them: "A tip for the next race. Only a shilling. I've tipped two winners today." His toes showed through his shoes'. After the fight Pinkie hides by some jerry-built house: 'the faintest sound of music from the Palace Pier bit, like an abscess, into his brain. . . the owner had come a long way to land up here . . . the small villa under the race-course was the best finish he could manage . . . the mortgaged home in the bottom; like the untidy tide-mark on a beach, the junk was piled up here and would never go farther. And the Boy hated him. He was nameless, faceless, but the Boy hated him'. Perhaps Pinkie senses that this derelict contemporary junk is an image of himself. Certainly it is an appropriate image for much of the novel. Perversity and squalor loom large in its basic theme—the confrontation of two levels of being or of two sets of values, the placing of the spiritual against the fleshly, the religious against the secular, the realm of Good and Evil against the world of Right and Wrong. And always these abstractions or non-material forces are presented in palpable human terms, the metaphysical is involved in the physical; for example, the numbers of the winning horses are displayed to the waiting multitudes eager to be ransomed and blessed by Fortune, and those who have chosen (betted) well go up to communicate with the bookmakers and receive the means of life, aware though of the proximity of death and the princes of this world: 'the censer swung and the priest raised the Host, and the loud-speaker intoned the winners: "Black Boy. Memento Mori. General Burgoyne."'

Rose articulates this basic confrontation. She understands that she and Pinkie are of the realm of Good and Evil and at a different level and with different values from those of the world of Right and Wrong which Ida and nearly all the others inhabit. Those of Rose's and Pinkie's realm are more alive and human, and know evil and do evil and know goodness and some-times, by the grace of God, are good, while those like

Ida have not developed sufficiently to be able to discriminate and choose spiritually or even to be damned. Rose's scorn (aroused because the hurt and fallen youth to whom she is attached is being hounded so relentlessly for no good purpose) comes over powerfully, together with the telling paradox that the slight sixteen-year-old virgin who, in material terms, has been nowhere and done nothing, has more grasp of reality than the engaging and well-covered woman learned in the ways of the world and the appetites and comforts of the flesh: Rose exclaims, ' "It's Her . . . Asking questions. Soft as butter. What does she know about *us* ? . . . she doesn't know what a mortal sin is . . . Right and wrong. That's what she talks about . . . As if she knew." She whispered with contempt: "Oh, she won't burn. She couldn't burn if she tried." She might have been discussing a damp Catherine wheel . . . "I'd rather burn with you than be like Her." '

These confrontations are involved with the theme of the fugitive, the chases and escapes which course strongly through the novel. They are various, and the secular is interwoven with the religious. The crowds are pursuing pleasure and successful bets and the horses are pursuing each other and victory. But, more specifically and relevantly, Spicer is pursued by Pinkie and by Colleoni's men; Rose is pursued by Ida; and Pinkie is pursued by Ida and Hale's ghost, by Colleoni and his men, by his fears of sex and marriage, and by the love of Rose which is associated with the pity and mercy of God reluctant to let even the greatest sinner be lost.

Confrontation, flight (note the bird imagery) and pursuit, then, make up the main movement and pattern of the novel. Some examples of them and of other features have been pointed out in the first section of Part Four which seems to be the pivot of the novel. We should appreciate fully in what way this section is crucial, what leads up to it and what leads away from it, and realize also that each of the other scenes makes its singular contribution to the whole. So finely wrought is the novel that to understand its diversified yet harmonious texture, its tone and feeling, its intrinsic nature, it is necessary to consider much else— the kind of novel it is, for a start, how it fits in with and gains relevance and a broader appeal from the contemporary vogue for the crime-thriller.

Questions

1. Compare and contrast the two or three opening pages of 1, i with those of 4, i.

2. How are:
    (a)   Pinkie's youth and inexperience,
    (b)   his determination and ruthlessness,
    (c)   his obsession with 'the game', shown in Part Four?

3. How does Drewitt's speech differ from that of the other characters in Part Four, and why?

4. Imagine that you are Crab and write a report to Colleoni about what happened on the race-course in Part Four.

5. Select one or two scenes, anywhere in the novel, which you think are especially suitable for the cinema, and show how you would film them.

THE CRIME-THRILLER
and GRAHAM GREENE

When we say that *Brighton Rock* is a crime-thriller it is important to understand what is meant by this and to appreciate, as far as possible, why Graham Greene uses this form. It is, of course, very popular, and anyone who writes a really good crime-thriller is likely to make a lot of money out of the book, the paperback and the film and broadcast rights. No one but a block-head ever wrote except for money, Dr Johnson declares. There is something in this, and, no doubt, Graham Greene is pleased that his writings have made him a rich man. It is also pleasing to have a large audience. Every serious writer wishes to reach as many people as possible, so long as he can do so without blurring his vision or compromising his principles. He does not seek to restrict or confound but to emancipate and enrich. He writes as honestly and lucidly as he can, and if sometimes his work is hard to understand it is because of the nature of the experiences he is dealing with. Eliot's "Ash-Wednesday" and Yeats's "Byzantium" are as clear as possible; what each of them is consists exactly of those words in that order, nothing more or less. It happens, though, that sometimes writing seems so unusual in form, and so allusive, enigmatic or concentrated in matter that only a cultivated minority of readers can enjoy and comprehend it. This was felt to be the case with much of the great writing of the years 1910 to 1942. By the mid-nineteen-sixties, however, a good deal of this had been assimilated, and today secondary school pupils are reading it with more ease and comprehension than the professional reviewers who loudly gave vent to their bafflement and indignation on the first appearance of Hopkins, Lawrence, Eliot and Joyce.

Eliot, though, was apparently not content to be admired only by a cultivated minority. He sought to impress a wider audience, in plays such as *Murder in the Cathedral*, with a title like a crime-thriller, *Family Reunion*, employing the conventions of the whodunit (though it concerns not so much crime and punishment as sin and expiation) and *The Cocktail Party* with its engaging surface of modish intrigue and psycho-analysis. Eliot speaks of the various levels of significance in *Hamlet* and of the various kinds of satisfaction they provide or needs they meet. The same is true of Shakespeare's other plays, and, at another grade of quality and intensity, of Eliot's plays. Each operates on more than one level simultaneously and communicates with diverse individuals in an audience.

Something similar applies to Graham Greene's novels. In reading them groups of people, usually of differing tastes, share an experience; the audience for Raymond Chandler and the audience for E. M. Forster are brought together. A degree of the rare quality of the Bible, mediaeval and Elizabethan drama, the ballads, John Bunyan, the novels of Dickens and the films of Charlie Chaplin which entertained, instructed and enriched mass audiences, is in Greene's novels; they are at once popular and serious. They use the commonest literary form of our day—the crime-thriller, and yet they present basic human and spiritual issues. The surface on which one contentedly moves or the level to which one burrows is a matter of choice—each may be enjoyed separately or together. Yet in Greene's novels there is always the chance that the reader after only the stock diversions of a crime-thriller may be led to deeper experience and insight. We get happily more than we bargained for. This is one of Greene's singular achievements, that he satisfies differing demands without failing or upsetting any one, that instead of stratifying or isolating he links diverse kinds of readers and that he sets up reverberations which give us the stimulus and the energy to go on exploring. In other words, his novels are a product of that imagination, described by Coleridge, which harmonizes and illuminates and fuses disparate entities into a new and greater whole.

There are various elements which make up the popular crime-thriller. It has so many ramifications and off-shoots, though, that a comprehensive and detailed account of it can hardly be supplied; there are numberless infinities of crime-thrillers, individual books, films and plays, most of them of little or no literary value. Nevertheless, many of them overlap or duplicate each other, have enough in common for some general features of the type to be discerned, or, rather, for us to be able to say, without defining precisely what the type is in the abstract, that where such and such features predominate in a piece of writing it is of the crime-thriller kind. This is what one means when one attaches the label 'crime-thriller' to some of Greene's writings, not that they are identical with the rest of their kind—no good piece of writing is this, no matter how exactly it corresponds to the type— but that they display important features which loom large in most crime-thrillers. Unlike most of them, however, Greene's writings use these features in an adult way (providing not only diversion and excitement but also insight) and they are combined with other most uncommon qualities to become distinctive pieces of literature.

The crime-thriller is made up of violent, sometimes melodramatic, situations and action, intrigue and mystery, suspense, treachery and sudden reversals and death, in a mechanized hard-shell, soft centre urban existence, glittering, restless, tainted and transitory yet seeming at times to represent an enduring condition of mankind. These factors, in varying degrees, help towards the creation of the central theme of the crime-thriller—the theme of the man on the run, the hunted and the hunter, the fugitive and the avenger. This theme of pursuit, with all its related concerns of crime or sin, double-cross or betrayal, pay-off or expiation, in a fallen world, is salient in Greene's fiction. It comes in various shapes, in the comparatively simple form of a man fleeing across the country or a killer escaping in a train, in the more subtle form of a famous architect escaping from cosmopolitan success to a leper colony in the Congo or of a journalist seeking to remain merely a reporter and to avoid the responsibilities of leader-writing, and, finally, in a profound form, which encompasses all the others, of a sinner, tempted by virtue, in terror-stricken flight from the mercy of God, the Hound of Heaven.

One of Greene's 'juvenilia' *The Man Within* (1929), set in the early nineteenth century, is concerned with crime—smuggling—and the main character, Andrews, after being involved in a scuffle between smugglers and excise-men, in which an excise-man is killed, flees across the Sussex Downs and is given refuge by Elizabeth. He is strangely moved by her, she appeals to the finer man within him, and she persuades him to go back to take part in the trial at which his evidence will be crucial. He does this, although it is very dangerous. He becomes entangled with Lucy who represents the Flesh just as Elizabeth represents the Spirit. Feeling guilty at having betrayed Elizabeth, Andrews speeds back to her and is forgiven, but the other smugglers also feeling betrayed close in. Elizabeth is murdered, and Andrews revolted by 'a terror of life, of going on soiling himself and repenting and soiling himself again', confesses to the murder, partly in order to save a comrade on whom the guilt would otherwise fall; and then, surprisingly feeling happy and at peace (because the better man within is becoming dominant) commits suicide.

Movement is nearly everything in *Stamboul Train* (1932). For most of the time the characters are hurtling across Europe at express speed, and each of them is, in some way or another, either pursuer or pursued or both. These flights are from cold or boredom or racial hostility to good food, a new job or a business deal, from a dying love relationship to a fresh one. The more sustained expressions of them occur in Grünlich, a hardened criminal, escaping after robbery and murder, and proud of being a killer yet fearful of the consequences, and in Dr. Czinner, driven by a strong social conscience, away from an aimless but comfortable existence in England, to lead a workers' rising in his native land. He is recognized by the secret police and hounded to death. Coral, a pretty but lonely chorus-girl, is involved in his arrest and attempt to escape. She, however, is rescued, after a couple of very hectic car chases, by Mabel Warren, a journalist and a ruthless hunter after a scoop. Coral is sought by Mabel, who is a Lesbian, while Mabel's former companion escapes from her and becomes engaged with a rich young Jew who briefly had sexual relationships with Coral. This is a sketch of an ingenious but clear and fast-moving story packed with quick sense impressions that cohere meaningfully. Although, moving at this speed and level, there is little detailed or rounded characterization, human insights are provided with irony and compassion.

In *The Confidential Agent* (1939) the main character, 'D', is seen more fully and intimately, and almost all the novel is presented from his point of view. He comes to England to obtain coal for the use of his side in a civil war. He is ruthlessly hunted by his enemies and betrayed by his comrades, until the murder of Else, a skinny, pathetic fourteen-year old servant (similar to Rose) transforms him into a hunter. He avenges her, then pursued by the police, dashes north to set off a strike of coal-miners before escaping to the Continent. Greene's swift inventiveness is amazing.

In *The Man Within*, *Stamboul Train* and *The Confidential Agent* (together with *A Gun for Sale* and *Brighton Rock*, to be examined more fully later) Greene shows himself a master of the crime-thriller. The stock ingredients are there—the pursuit, the unbroken physical action, providing surprise after surprise, sudden disclosures, reversals and appearances, the betrayals and disguises, the arrival of the avenger or the police in the nick of time, and the climax with people being appropriately saved or captured or killed. To obtain these effects in a short space not only must the style be spare—descriptions brief, sentences pithy, speech curt—but character must often be subordinated to action; the physical results of violence and intrigue are shown but little else. There is hardly scope for reflection or subtlety, for the placing of motives or consequences in a psychological context, for the cultivated play of intelligence or the fine assessment of principles and values. That Greene is able to use the stock ingredients in such a way as to make fruitful connections with the spheres of mental and moral activity is one indication of his very high capacities. Inevitably, however, the melodramatic elements loom large in his earlier writings and he calls some of them 'entertainments'. But as he develops, the enduring human and moral concerns of the serious novelist predominate. Nevertheless, the amazing readability, the hold on the concrete and moving world of everyday, the gripping nature of his work, persist; and the blending of passion and precision, the economy of wording which produces a range and depth of effect resembling poetry (Greene's 'world' has been linked with that of Webster and the Jacobean dramatists), increases in power and significance. So, too, does the theme of pursuit.

The Power and the Glory (1940) consists entirely of the unremitting pursuit of a priest in a South American state where the Church has been outlawed by the Communists in power. At the beginning there is a contrast between him and Tench, a dentist, immersed in decay, the decay of his life and surroundings, the decay of the country and the decay of teeth, who longs to escape but has not the means. The priest has the means and the opportunity easily to escape several times, but his sense of vocation keeps him there, though hunted constantly. Outwardly he is a bad priest, drunken, squalid, a liar and adulterer, and he appears to do no good to anyone. In the end he allows himself to be betrayed in going to an American gangster, a Catholic, mortally wounded while on the run. The fugitive priest is caught and executed, dying wretchedly, believing that his life has been a failure and realizing (too late, he thinks) 'that there was only one thing that counted—to be a saint'. But at the same time the grace of martyrdom which has also been following him catches him and becomes his, and he is set free from all decay.

The chief character in *The Heart of the Matter* (1948), Scobie, seeks escape from a world that has become soiled and from the intolerable complications and demands of love that is hurting his wife and his mistress. Pity for them pursues him at every turn. In a sense he wants nothing for himself, his ultimate happiness is 'being in darkness, alive, with the rain falling, without love or pity', but in another sense that peace he seeks ('A condition of complete simplicity') costs not less than everything. In grasping at it through suicide, he is fleeing from God, pushing Him away, battering God in the face, but God, like a punch-drunk boxer continues to come up for more. He is also betraying God: he senses another wrong and another victim (not his wife or his mistress), and the 'cocks began to crow for the false dawn'. The novel has this epigraph: 'le pécheur est au cœur même de chrétienté . . . Nul n'est aussi compétent que le pécheur en matière de chrétienté. Nul, si ce n'est le saint'; it is central in Greene and it is from Charles Péguy whom the old priest trying to comfort Rose at the end of

Brighton Rock refers to. For Scobie, like Rose and like the priest in *The Power and the Glory*, is willing to die and be damned for the sake of those he loves. But God does not give up. Even as Scobie is dying he hears a call for help, the cry of a victim, and he tries to respond. It is God still pursuing, between the stirrup and the ground. Whether Scobie found grace in this final extremity Greene does not say, for the priest to whom Scobie's wife, a Catholic believing that Scobie is damned for committing suicide, goes, declares that no one can comprehend God's infinite mercy.

In *The End of the Affair* (1951) Bendrix pursues Sarah, the wife of a civil servant, and possesses her. Later Bendrix is stunned and apparently dead in an air-raid. After this she eludes him. Suspecting another lover, Bendrix puts a private investigator on her track. To his amazement he finds she has become involved with God. During the air-raid she had vowed to God to renounce Bendrix if he recovered. She is trying to keep her vow and in doing so leaping into faith. Deriding all this, Bendrix again pursues her, but she, though deeply loving him, avoids him. Bendrix becomes more aggressive in his pursuit, at last forcing her, though ill, to flee from him one cold wet night to a church. She catches pneumonia and dies. Certain things happen that could be interpreted as miracles, and Bendrix is driven most unwillingly to the conclusion that his rival, God, has made Sarah a saint. And then Bendrix realizes with horror that, partly through the influence of Sarah on whom he continually broods, God is pursuing him, and the novel ends with Bendrix protesting so much that he hates God that it seems that he, too, will in due course be captured.

This image of Man on the run through a stricken and flashy world, glittering with corruption, pursued by a God who never gives up, is at the heart of Greene. It occurs, of course, in other writers in different generations, and most obviously perhaps and resembling Greene, though in another style, in the remarkable poem by Francis Thompson, a Catholic, 'The Hound of Heaven'. In Greene it is seen most clearly, and its implications, religious, human and social, are most thoroughly explored, in the three novels just touched on here.

It is by no means so palpable and penetrating in *The Quiet American* (1955). There are, however, traces. They are associated with pity which can, in Greene, either be a destructive force or may lead to compassion and humility. In the naïve American, Pyle, pity is allied with ignorant good-will, impetuous physical courage and insensitivity. People like Pyle, Fowler cries, should carry bells so that they can be avoided like lepers or should be destroyed as dangerous animals. In Fowler pity takes another course and shape. He tries, in direct contrast to Pyle, to avoid becoming really involved with people or nations; he wishes to be a mere reporter. But gradually through his feeling for the poor and afflicted, through his longing for peace (somewhat like Scobie's) and ironically through the intrigues of Pyle which cause him to do wrong (the elimination of Pyle), in order to prevent a much greater wrong (the massacre of the innocent), he is led to become *engagé*, committed or involved, to become a leader-writer and take up a moral position. Fowler is pursued through *not* experiencing lasting loss and suffering; he is got at by being given all he sought, his cup of blessings is filled and running over. This produces, however, a deep sense of inadequacy and personal guilt, of having received much more than he deserves, and he wishes profoundly that there existed someone to whom he could say that he was sorry. He is outside the Church, however, and so does not have its guidance towards this 'someone' or towards discriminating between crime and sin, between rewards and blessings, between right and wrong and good and evil. The Hound of Heaven seems a long way off, but He moves in mysterious ways, and at the end He is, at least, stirring.

The main character, Querry, in *A Burnt-Out Case* (1961) is certainly on the run. His flight seems, in a way, a grotesque parody of the glossy travel advertisements urging people to flee the dismal, frigid and artificial north for the bright, fecund and natural south. Querry, the fever for success burnt-out in him, is abandoning a career as an international architect and various sophisticated possessions and relationships. His fame and worldly affairs have gone bad on him, and as he moves deeper on an old Congo paddle-steamer into one of the darkest and steamiest parts of Africa, he endures and even welcomes a sort of purgatory. Forsaking all, he hopes to lose his self-regard and to find peace—and Pendélé, a primitive folk Eden (hinted at by Querry's servant, Deo Gratias, a cured leper, a burnt-out case) where there is singing and dancing, natural rites which may revitalize our meretricious world. His is a journey towards the point at which our childhood went astray, unconsciously perhaps towards that condition in which we are as little children and may inherit the Kingdom of Heaven. But still the world pursues—in the shape (much resembling Ida Arnold of *Brighton Rock*) of a gross and self-indulgent but very determined journalist avid to grasp or concoct the 'true story', in his highly-paid jargon, behind Querry's flight from civilization. Querry's retreat is also assailed by a planter, Rycker, one of the smug, pious, formalistic, self-centred Catholics Greene is so adept at placing, and by Rycker's pretty young wife, an innocent abroad (like Pyle), single-minded and disingenuous, and therefore very dangerous, who compromises the guiltless Querry. The intrigues of these three bring about Querry's death, though not before he has gained some illumination from the leper colony, the priests, the African patients and Dr. Colin, an atheist and a kind of 'secular saint', the opposite of Rycker.

The foregoing brief survey of eight representative pieces of fiction shows (it is hoped) how vital and central the theme of the pursuit—the core of the crime-thriller—is in Greene. This theme is often associated with betrayal and sometimes with other features of the crime-thriller, such as swift changes of role or identity or the producing of a climax by shooting. In his mature novels Greene is grappling with funda-mental human and spiritual issues, moving down innumerable and labyrinthine ways, and in them the main features of the crime-thriller are so subtly intertwined as not to be so discernible as in earlier writings of more modest aims. *A Gun for Sale* (1936) is probably the best example of a pure crime-thriller, almost entirely free from ranging undertones or resonances, and through it the main features of the genre may readily be observed. It is also close to *Brighton Rock*.

Raven, the main character in *A Gun for Sale*, resembles Pinkie. He has been in crime on race-courses and elsewhere and he was one of the gang who slashed Kite to death. Hell lay about Raven in his infancy. When he was six his father was hanged, his mother afterwards committed suicide with a household knife, collapsing across the kitchen table, the blood all over her dress, and he was then brought up in an institution. Through a premature experience of brutality and evil which extinguished his innocence, and branded with a hare-lip, he was conditioned to resentment and destruction and became a hardened killer ready to do what his employers ordered without any feeling. Davis who hires Raven is a fat carnal man, similar to Ida Arnold. He is an agent for Sir Marcus, a millionaire armament-maker, who (like Colleoni) lives in great wealth and respectability away from the crime and squalor and pain which he ordains and benefits from. He wishes to give his vast business concern, Midland Steel, a new lease of life, and so he secretly organizes a war-scare. Raven is ordered to assassinate the mild and liberal War Minister of a Central European state.

The novel opens in a most gripping manner with Raven doing the job with his usual unfeeling professional competence. But returning to England, he is betrayed on all sides. Davis pays him in stolen and marked bank-notes and immediately the police are on his trail. His landlord and a handicapped servant girl he has tried to befriend, mock and inform on him, and the crook doctor whom he is paying well to operate and remove the incriminating hare-lip calls the police. His position is similar to that of 'D' in *The Confidential Agent*, ironically an agent in whom no one has confidence, who has only limited confidence in himself and his cause and whose confidential mission soon becomes widely known. Isolated and hunted, he has to use every resource to live from minute to minute. Raven too is quite alone, and ready to declare with Pinkie that he will be driven to carve the whole boiling. He resolves to get Davis at least. And the various inter-related pursuits which so excitingly make up this entertainment are well under way.

Raven shadows Davis by train to Nottwich. Anne, fiancée of Mather, the detective seeking Raven, is on the train. In Nottwich she becomes tangled with Raven and learns from him of Davis's part in the assassination. She realizes that unless the truth is made known the world war which she greatly fears will break out. She makes up to Davis, trying to trap him, but he is too cunning for her and almost murders her. Raven rescues her but by now the police are closing in. Raven is able to tell her all, and she, though horrified at him, feels pity too, and deciding that he must be helped to his revenge so that war may be prevented, she puts the police on a false trail long enough for Raven to get at and kill Sir Marcus and Davis just before he is shot by the police.

The cinema clichés about 'breathless excitement, hairbreadth escapes and thrillpacked action' may certainly be applied to *A Gun for Sale*. The handling of time and movement is especially notable. From beginning to end everything has to be done in a hurry. Raven has to get Davis before the police get him—and the police are never more than an hour or two away; the truth about the assassination must be broadcast before the bombers take off—and the nations are

mobilizing (and air-raid precautions being taken) as
the news-flashes show. This sense of time rapidly
running out chimes in exactly with the swift and
stealthy manœuvres of the hunters and hunted.
Sometimes one or other of the pursuers loses the trail
or is baffled momentarily and the fleeing creature may
lie low gasping for breath, but the tension persists.
And never more so than in a bizarre scene in the
Hitchcock manner, using a harmless public meeting or
festivity as a centre for crime, as in the British Council
lecture in *The Third Man*, the 'Entrenationo' tea party
in *The Confidential Agent* and the charity-fair in *The
Ministry of Fear*. Here it is a church jumble sale. Raven,
temporarily out of touch, spots a woman with Anne's
handbag and follows her and is himself then followed
by Mather who, equally at a loss, had also dropped
into the jumble sale, and identified Raven by his
hare-lip.

The various flights and pursuits, each with its own
aims and motives, the diverse shiftings and reversals,
changes of roles and loyalties, are all intricately related
and woven together and wrought to a climax which
resolves each satisfactorily. It is brought about by one
of the minor sequences of chase and escape and surprise
and reversal which merge into the general pattern.
This concerns Buddy Ferguson, a flabby and loud-
mouthed medical student, who puts on bravado to hide
his fears and insufficiencies and leads a group of
loutish students to debag another student, their social
and intellectual superior, and to wreck his room.
Swaggering after this, Buddy sees Raven, and thinking
he has an easy victim chases him. But hunter becomes
hunted, he is quickly cut down to size by the slight

determined man, and himself now a victim has to hand over all his clothes to Raven who disguised in them and in Buddy's gas-mask—everyone on the streets must wear a gas-mask during air-raid practice—is enabled to penetrate to the heart of the Midland Steel offices for the final reckoning with Davis and Sir Marcus.

He kills them all right—much to the delight of Sir Marcus's personal valet. Even at the end there are betrayals and surprises and those deft incidental touches which make Greene's writings so singularly convincing and penetrating. Economic necessity has forced this valet to spend years tending the ailing body of the mean and nasty old Sir Marcus, and now his suppressed loathing bursts forth into awful joy as he sees someone doing what he has longed to do but daren't.

But judgement is near for Raven too. And in this crisis he is (like other main figures in Greene's fiction) bewildered and disabled by pity. Perceiving that this is a world where the tender and sensitive are crushed, he has become callous and icy and built round him an armour of suspicion and hatred. Earlier, walking through the snowy streets in a vain attempt to keep warm, he heard a record being played in Anne's room; the snow flakes 'went on falling, melting into slush on the pavement, the words of a song dropped from the lit room on the third floor, the scrape of a used needle.

"They say that's a snowflower
    A man brought from Greenland,
    I say it's the lightness, the coolness, the whiteness
    Of your hand."

The man hardly paused; he went on down the street, walking fast; he felt no pain from the chip of ice in his breast.' But later, getting acquainted with Anne, he is touched by her kindness and courage. She sings the song. 'He said "I've heard that tune" . . . he remembered a dark night and a cold wind and hunger and the scratch of a needle. It was as if something sharp and cold were breaking in his heart with great pain. He sat there under the sink with the automatic and began to cry.' Like Pinkie (though not in a perverted way) he is moved by the combination of a popular sentimental song and an unselfish, sympathetic woman. Lacking Pinkie's dimension of evil he does not ward it off, though all his experience urges him to remain hard: 'he wasn't used to any taste that wasn't bitter on the tongue. He had been made by hatred; it had constructed him into this thin smoky murderous figure in the rain . . . He had a sudden terrified conviction that he must be himself now as never before, if he was to escape. It was not tenderness that made you quick on the draw.' Then, having saved her life, and appalled at the treachery of Davis and Sir Marcus, being alone with her in the railway shed, surrounded by fog and the police, in a kind of confessional, he melts through her warmth, his armour is pierced by her compassion and by what she tells him about the Minister he shot who was a good man who had risen from squalid origins, similar to Raven's (his father had been a thief and his mother had committed suicide). He trusts her and tells her about his hideous life and crimes. (This is another example of the way in which in Greene confession may promote moral rehabilitation but also physical peril.) She does not seem horrified but helps him to elude the police, and he is filled with strange emotions that there is now one person whom he trusts and who trusts him. But in the get-away a policeman is killed, and Anne, very upset at this, betrays Raven to the police. They arrive fortunately too late to save Sir Marcus and Davis but in time to kill Raven who is unable to act with his usual skill, because at the realization that she too has betrayed him he is terribly sickened and suddenly tired of life; allowing pity and tenderness past his defences and into him leads to his destruction.

This characteristic concern with pity and betrayal, and the passing reference to the Christmas cribs and Raven's recollection of the story taught him in the wretched institution of his childhood which rouses a crude sympathy for 'the little bastard' double-crossed by Judas, these are the only traces of a religious theme in *A Gun for Sale*. Basically it is an excellent crime-thriller. Because of this, because, though notable in itself, it is near enough to the ordinary crime-thriller to serve as a model, it is a book very suitable for consideration along with *Brighton Rock*, both for its similarities and for its differences. Simply, *A Gun for Sale* shares with *Brighton Rock* the main features (though with differing levels of intensity and significance) of the crime-thriller—the glamour and squalor of people fighting on the fringes of respectability, making up their own brittle and meretricious society with its slickness and violence and shadiness—the world of right and wrong. But it does not have the metaphysical elements, the concern with spritual good and evil, of *Brighton Rock*. Further detailed comparisons and contrasts of the two books might well be made, but there is scope now only to focus on *Brighton Rock* and to specify some of the features of the crime-thriller which it embodies.

There are more instances of flight and pursuit in *Brighton Rock* than in any other of Greene's writings and perhaps than in any other work of fiction of merit. A list, not necessarily exhaustive, would include the following: the flights of Hale and of Spicer from Pinkie to escape death (both unsuccessful), (ironically, the flight of Kolley Kibber from the crowds seeking the prize is successful), the flight of Rose from Ida to escape worldly forces assailing her love and spiritual values (successful), the flight of Pinkie from marriage (unsuccessful) and from Colleoni and his gang to escape further carving and disgrace (successful) and Pinkie's flight from Ida (and Hale's ghost) and, incidentally, the police, to escape from punishment, although he is driven to worse retribution. Then there are two cases which are partly successful: Drewitt's flight from his wife and his shady practice, and Cubitt's flight from Pinkie (which is a bizarre parody of a soul turning from the devil to God) and his going to Colleoni for forgiveness and a place in his kingdom. And, more important, there is Pinkie's flight from God's mercy and love, which seems successful, and his insidious pushing of Rose towards damnation which she supports by fleeing from God to be damned with him, and this is just prevented by the final pursuit by Ida, Dallow and the policeman. They get there at the right time for the classic crime-thriller climax where characters die or are saved appropriately and all the various pursuits are satisfactorily resolved. There is just, perhaps, one last twist of the knife—Rose's rapid walk 'in the thin June sunlight towards the worst horror of all'— the recorded voice of Pinkie cursing her with utter venom. Will this curse always pursue her?

In crime-thrillers there are often mysteries which have to be solved by the gathering and study of clues, the tapping of people and the tracking of suspects. Sometimes this is done (as in *A Gun for Sale* and *Z Cars*) by the regular police; sometimes (as in *The Man from UNCLE* and, to some extent, Bond, and, in parody, in Greene's *Our Man in Havana*) by organizations with the latest and most astounding machinery and appliances for operating all over the world; and sometimes by private investigators, charming and eccentric amateurs, such as Sherlock Holmes and Sir Peter Wimsey, or those who tend today to be slick and hardened professionals, with marked physical strength and dexterity and sexual virtuosity, sophisticated allure and endless gimmickry. Greene's investigator, Ida, is different from all these, yet she ably performs most of their functions. She alone suspects something sinister about Hale's death. She goes through the set procedures, attending the funeral, questioning the last people to see the dead man alive, consulting her authority (the ouija board), being brushed off by the police, but not wavering, a sticker. She interviews barmen, piecing bits together from her experience of that significant border-land where respectability and crime merge—the public-houses, cheap lodgings, big hotels and race-courses—where people relax from their responsibilities and see life. She discusses the case with her timid and feeble associate and has her sexual diversion with him (a telling contrast with Bond's grandiose affairs), but immediately she is on the hunt again, probing, bribing, lying, threatening, getting into the H.Q. of the big shot (the Cosmopolitan), cajoling with drink and sentiment a dissatisfied member of the gang into betrayal, sending false messages to confuse her quarry and to make him act rashly, and then at the right time turning on the heat and helping to drive him to disaster. Ida certainly is formidable. Her only deficiency—lack of the sinews of war—is sportingly supplied by her client after his death paying the fee, £250 winnings on Black Boy. Otherwise she is impregnable, through her over-ripe sensuality and easy tolerance, through her relish for fun and natural failings, through the 'compassion and comprehension' she carried 'about her like a rank cheap perfume'; most of all through her disarming ease coupled with a ruthless determination to put things right, to make those who did wrong suffer for it. She is helped (as investigators invariably are) by the mistakes of the criminals. Pinkie makes two misjudgements: he under-rates Rose's love and Ida's malice and resource.

Sometimes in order to break the criminal, pressure is put on his girl-friend. But here Pinkie has his greatest strength and the avenue to rehabilitation (if he knew it). Rose is different from the usual gangster's moll (well exemplified in Sylvie and Judy). She is not a wanton, a vamp, a sentimentalist or a betrayer. She is faithful to her man, more so than any other woman in Greene's fiction (except strangely perhaps Sarah in *The End of the Affair*). Her love for Pinkie is unlike that in most crime-thrillers, where it becomes a matter of crude appetites, fleeting and vain, prurient or sentimental. Such desires are part of the damaging disregard for tenderness and genuine feeling in crime-thrillers. The characters assume a tough exterior but they are soft inside. Stress is laid on 'manly' physical power and skills but when, inevitably, feeling, 'romantic interest', appears, sloppiness quickly prevails. This is shown most amusingly and tellingly in Cubitt. His gifts of 'a tiny doll's commode in the shape of a radio set . . . and a mustard pot shaped like a lavatory seat' have been rejected and he has quarrelled with Pinkie. He becomes maudlin, feeling 'the need of a deep sentimental affection, orange blossoms and a cuddle in a corner. His great paw yearned for a sticky hand'. He buys from a machine a penny 'True Love' card, the most banal sentiment, and is deeply moved; 'it is class, literature . . . Loved and lost. Tragic griefs flamed under his carrot hair'. In this horrible emotional mess, yearning to be soothed at a woman's breast, he comes across the warm, enveloping Ida and soon betrays Pinkie.

This swing between callousness and mawkishness is, of course, a mark of the immaturity of the characters. Where they are not exposed but held up for admiration it is a mark of the immaturity of the book in which they appear. It is linked with the amazing stupidity of criminals in most crime-thrillers. Often they are mere straw puppets for the hero to show off against. They begin impressively with grandiose schemes or threats and the most ingenious machinations, but by the end they make the most elementary mistakes— failing to knock an enemy out properly, overlooking a way of escape, leaving a knife near a bound person, driving their cars or shooting badly, and instead of immediately killing the helpless hero and clearing out, gloatingly describing all their clever tricks until the rescuers arrive. By these standards Pinkie and his gang seem efficient—but only up to a point. Pinkie behaves with little more understanding than a seventeen-year-old can be expected to have and the rest of them, past their dubious best, are neither talented nor resourceful. It is in most ways a mediocre outfit, and in this it is much nearer the actualities of existence than are the figures of insubstantial cleverness and glamour in most crime-thrillers. Moreover, Greene is able to indicate by the gap between the modest capacities and attainments of Pinkie's gang and Pinkie's immense aspirations how boundless is Pinkie's pride—and this is what sets him apart (for he would defeat not only Colleoni but God) and makes him more menacing than any criminal who operates, however grandly, only in the secular sphere.

With this gross underrating of intellect and feeling in most crime-thrillers there is a corresponding obsession with things and machinery, with novel and astounding (and barely credible) devices for speed, communications and death. Such dehumanizing fantasies do not occur in *Brighton Rock*; there the things used are ordinary—the battered car and the telephone call and the letter; guns are not mentioned, and, apart from the bottle of vitriol (which recoils on its possessor) the only weapons are razors. These facts link *Brighton Rock* with recognizable actualities. It does not, unlike the novels of Ian Fleming, fly into regions less human and more insubstantial than those of fairy-stories, or even of Walt Disney. The murder of Hale is carried out imaginatively and plausibly with the means to hand—a stick of Brighton rock is thrust down his throat. In such simple ways and by the power of his writing, Greene makes crime more horrible and real than the highly intricate and sophisticated machinations in Fleming where there is such a showy immersion in technical details and glossy gadgets that the facts of human joy and suffering and death are almost ignored. This is one of the points of moral superiority of Greene over Fleming and his like. Greene's characters, no matter how viciously or strangely they behave, possess human characteristics, arousing terror and compassion and making us freshly aware of the boredom and the horror and the glory of being alive. They are not things, not dazzling fleshly shapes, flashing through routines, though in startlingly ingenious postures and situations, and then being discarded in the cause of the hero. The victory in crime-thrillers is for right over wrong—as interpreted by the authorities or (alarmingly) by the private code of Superman or a secret organization. James Bond, like Ida, could not burn. Greene embraces not only the realm of the crime-thriller but also the realm of good and evil. To use Coleridge's classic distinction: Fleming's work is of fancy, Greene's of imagination.

Questions

1. Test the validity of the above comments by comparing one or two novels by Ian Fleming (or by any notable writer of crime-thrillers) with *Brighton Rock*.

2. Compare and contrast Raven, Anne, Davis and Sir Marcus in *A Gun for Sale* with Pinkie, Rose, Ida and Colleoni in *Brighton Rock*.

3. Select any one section (other than 4, i) in *Brighton Rock* and show precisely how the theme of pursuit is carried on.

4. Imagine that you are the ghost of Hale speaking to Ida and explain all you did and felt from the time of your arrival in Brighton to your murder.

5. Imagine that you are Spicer and write a letter to Sylvie describing your feelings and actions from the moments after Hale was murdered to the moment just before you too are murdered.

6. Consider the use of coincidences in a thriller: pick out examples of coincidence in *Brighton Rock;* could a thriller exist without coincidences? What makes coincidences acceptable or unacceptable?

STRUCTURE and NARRATIVE

In *Brighton Rock* the facts that make up the mystery and provide a solution to it are very skilfully made available—sufficiently gradually to stimulate and challenge us but not too much to perplex us unduly. With increasing curiosity we gather the pieces and put them together. Our reading is creative. We come to understand the background and what sets the action off—that because of Hale, Kite was killed by Colleoni's mob—and we are impelled to find out what happens next.

The novel is instantly arresting. We want to know why they mean to murder Hale, and if and how they can manage it. In the exhilarating movement of gay life (the active verbs and the rapid varied cinematic views are effective) Hale seems like a fugitive in a jungle. He doesn't belong—because on a holiday he is working and feels not happy but doomed, and also because he has raised himself a bit, so when he is nostalgically drawn to the fleshly refuge of Ida his smattering of psychology holds him proudly back, taunting; 'back to the womb . . . be a mother to you'. But not for long. Pride and evil infinitely larger than his bear down upon him and he staggers in increasing terror from the experienced Ida to the ingenuous banalities of Molly and Delia (there is grim comedy in the meeting of the desperate Hale, the deadly Pinkie and the foolish coy girls with their cry: 'Now we can make a proper party'). Then he is back with Ida and she is becoming concerned when she goes into the ladies' lavatory briefly and Hale is lost.

Deft indications of time are given which show that

47

the murder took place just after 1-30. In the second section, Pinkie at 1-45, quite unmoved, blasphemously says a prayer, 'Hail Mary . . . in the hour of our death' to the glassy dolls like Virgins, shoots six bulls-eyes and establishes an alibi in the booth and another in the tea-room, while Spicer leaves a Kolley Kibber card in Snow's to suggest Hale died after two. Now after the hectic opening movements the gang are at lunch. They are not impressive, and already Spicer is getting into trouble, unable to eat, 'grey-haired and sick'. Pinkie shows himself a leader by coolly going to Snow's. He quickly realizes that Rose may be dangerous, and concealing his dislike declares with more truth than he knows that she and he have things in common. In the third section the focus is on Ida. A chat in a pub (like a confessional) reveals something amiss. Her sentimentality is aroused. She cunningly inquires and follows up clues, and her self-righteous determination to punish the wrong-doer becomes stronger. She conducts a bizarre ceremony, a secular parody of the Mass, where the Board represents the Host and the Word, and Old Crowe represents a guardian of the shrine with passion only for the Board which he fondles. Concentrating devoutly, Ida communicates with the Board and with the departed Hale, and gains strength and inspiration for her mission. Funny and perhaps pathetic though this scene may appear, there are faiths (however ridiculous or perverse) that move mountains, and by the end it is obvious that Ida will be a dangerous adversary: ' "I'm going to make those people sorry they was ever born." She drew in breath luxuriously . . . "I believe in right and wrong" . . . she said: "it's going to be exciting, it's going to be fun,

it's going to be a bit of life, Old Crowe", giving the
highest praise she could give to anything.' (1, iii).

By the end of Part One the leading characters and
issues have clearly and grippingly emerged, and the
novel is well wound-up for developing action. Each of
the three sections presented the viewpoint of one
character, Hale, Pinkie and Ida. The same method
continues for the rest of the novel providing a sequence
of individual points of view, as if from a battery of
movie cameras, though penetrating into mental spheres
where cameras actually can't go, each cutting across
and reinforcing or commenting on or contrasting with
the others.

The consideration that the imagination is a moral
agent is central in literature. It is given support in
Part Two by the fact that Pinkie's strength comes from
his lack of imagination: 'He couldn't see through other
people's eyes or feel with their nerves,' (2, i) (just as
Macbeth's capacity for evil increases as his imagination
withers). But music could move him, and after warning
Spicer that a second murder is sometimes necessary to
tidy up after a previous one, and warning Rose to
keep silent, he reveals that link between stale romantic
tunes, vitriol and pain that produces his peculiar
sexual feeling. A crooner sings, holding the microphone
'tenderly as if it were a woman, swinging it gently . . .
wooing it with his lips while from the loudspeaker
under the gallery his whisper reverberated hoarsely
over the hall, like a dictator announcing victory, like
the official news following a long censorship . . . The
crowd stood at attention . . . dead quiet.' (2, i). The
music 'gets' Pinkie and he surrenders, characteristically
not to the human, but to the brazen, inhuman voice,

the stock words, 'love, nightingale', stirring in his brain like poetry, and he caresses the vitriol bottle in his pocket, then, sensing a menace—marriage, bed, vitriol in his face (which all happen)—he turns his venom on Rose, seeking his satisfaction in hurting her. But she suffers for his sake and doesn't squeal, and it is no pleasure. Pain, however, is real, can be depended on, like Hell, he asserts, when each has learned that the other is a Catholic. 'And Heaven too', Rose puts in anxiously. 'Maybe', says Pinkie indifferently. So vividly the stuff and shape of their relationship is clearly indicated.

The venom appears ferociously at Spicer's suggestion that the gang should lay off, and especially at his joke that Pinkie might marry Rose. Spicer does not see that he is putting himself into peril. The reason why Pinkie is chief also appears. His exclusive concern for himself which frees him from scruple and bestows craft and even a kind of courage enables him to handle Brewer's refusal to pay. Again it is the hurt to his pride (the suggestion that he go in with Colleoni) that prompts him to slash. There is irony in Brewer's cry as the blood runs down his face that he has protection. Certainly he is paying for it—twice—but hardly getting it (though he will be avenged on the race-course). This scene shows the crude squalor and cowardice of Pinkie's operations, and they are contrasted with the opulence and ease of Colleoni when Pinkie visits him in the Cosmopolitan. Colleoni, though, is not much better than Pinkie, and he takes fewer risks—his carvings and dirty work are done and his alibis fixed by underlings. His wealth arises from the same vicious sources and his surroundings, though the reverse of squalid, appear decadent. But he is manifestly success-ful. This rankles deeply with Pinkie and so do Colleoni's advice and patronizing manner, which are echoed by the police who are put on to Pinkie by Colleoni. In this section Pinkie's pride has been sorely hurt. He has heard of things he doesn't understand; he has been made aware of his sexual limitations; he has had to appear in public with a despised polony whom he was not able even to make cry with pain, and his marriage with her has been considered a possibility. Four times (by Spicer, Brewer, Colleoni and the police inspector) he has been advised to pack up because he is not big enough for the job. These are severe and sustained assaults, but they are against the one part of himself that is indomitable. They feed rather than diminish his pride, for it is Satanic, as is shown by the allusion to the glory of the fallen angel, coupled with the superb reversal of Wordsworth's *Immortality Ode*. He aspires more instead of less, not marking (though the reader can) the immense gap between his aspirations and his resources:

> There was poison in his veins, though he grinned and bore it. He had been insulted. He was going to show the world. They thought because he was only seventeen . . . he jerked his narrow shoulders back at the memory that he'd killed his man, and these bogies who thought they were clever weren't clever enough to discover that. He trailed the clouds of his own glory after him: hell lay about him in his infancy. He was ready for more deaths. (2, ii).

Part Three shows Ida beginning her campaign. She needs 'sinews of war', so she backs Black Boy with

Tate, appropriately like a large toad, whose servile responses on the telephone to Colleoni show where the power lies. The barman also believes the kid hasn't a chance and when he points out Pinkie in the street, she sees only 'a boy in a shabby suit' unworthy of her attention. (3, i). But, to a reader, Pinkie's immense ambition is again marked by contrast with his inconspicuous appearance; just as the Tempter is often most potent when he appears insignificant. Still, forces are gathering against him and Ida is learning fast. She gets nothing, however, voluntarily out of Rose. At first, Rose is friendly, expressing naïvely her pleasure in her wretched job and revealing how little she expects. But when Ida probes, she closes up; yet artlessly she shows she is lying and mentions that the man ordered a Bass. Instantly Ida, who naturally remembers a man's preferences in drink, knows that it was not Hale who left the card. She blows confidently into the police-station, and, although, like most private investigators, she gets no support from officialdom, she resolves to press on, so long as Hale's tip is correct.

Ironically, as she stands by the pier turnstile where she last saw Hale and surveys 'the heavy traffic of her battlefield . . . marshalling her cannon fodder' (the people), the weakest point in her enemy is standing five yards from her—Spicer. He too, conventionally, has been drawn back to the scene of the crime. He is plagued, mentally and physically, fear 'like an abscess' jets poison through his nerves, his eyes are bloodshot, his bowels upset, there are eruptions round his mouth and nose, and a corn shoots pain through his whole body to his brain. News that Pinkie is at the police

station whirls him back to Billy's. At the head of the
stairs by the shaky banister looking down to the hall,
prophetically he affirms that he would rather die than
squeal. Rose on the phone, anxiously seeking Pinkie,
makes the torment worse. He blunders out, justifying,
arguing with, feeling sorry for himself 'a few tears of
self-pity pricking out of his dry ageing ducts'. (3, ii).
And in this confused and alarming state he is photo-
graphed. As he stands by the turnstile thinking that
he can spot the police if they begin investigations, he
does not know that he is doomed and that the avenging
agency is just by, nor—the final turn of this masterly
irony—does Ida know him.

Pinkie senses the doom of marriage closing in as he
goes into the country with Rose. Appalled, he twists
about, further sickened by the realization that it would
tie him again to the hated Nelson Place which he has
repudiated. He becomes so nasty that even Rose
protests, and he has to appease her. He realizes that he
may have to continue doing this, and feels that to
avoid it he would murder the world. Suddenly a more
immediate danger appears—the photo of Spicer,
guilt-ridden, for everyone to see. Pinkie has always
prevented his photo being taken and only a few hours
previously declared they should be banned. To which
the policeman replied: 'They caught a murderer once
in town with one of those snaps.' (2, ii). This remark is
perhaps recalled, chillingly. Rose, however, unaware of
the perilous implications, jokes that Spicer looks as if
he is afraid he will soon be dead. He will surely be
'among the immortals', a heterogeneous lot, listed in
three sentences (3, iii) which are a touchstone of
Greene's wonderful quality. This dispatching, since it

involves betrayal and cruelty is something Pinkie can
handle much better than love or sex. He gets to work
on Spicer. In a savage and most telling parody of a
lover blowing at a flower ('she loves me . . . she loves
me not' (3, iv)) Pinkie pulls off the legs and wings of a
leather-jacket and talks to Spicer, arranging for him
'to disappear', playing with him as with the insect,
looking 'for the second time in a few weeks' at a dying
man, speculating on Spicer's status in the next world—
'a glassy sea, a golden crown, old Spicer'. But he
'couldn't picture any eternity except in terms of pain',
and he says he is thinking of the races as they mean a
lot to him. They do to Ida also, and to others, in various
ways, some unexpected.

So, in Part Three, troubles press on Pinkie, but he
is seeking by one stroke to end them, with the dispatch
of Spicer, and the only uneasiness he has is the laugh
he thinks he hears as he is making the arrangements
with Colleoni.

By the opening of Part Four and going on the
race-course he is happy and confident—someone is
going to die for him. 'It is as easy as shelling peas'.
and he smiles at the double meanings of his remarks to
Spicer. How things go wrong—through the recoil of
treachery on himself and the ghostly influence of Hale—
has already been described.

Rose also is fighting, against a direct assault by the
shrewd and heavy Ida. Rose does not yield an inch,
and though she carries her courage 'with a kind of
comic inadequacy, like the little man in the bowler put
up by the management to challenge the strong man at
a fair' (4, iii), she beats off Ida. Even Pinkie, coming
along after the murder of Spicer and peering in, is

strangely moved and senses that she belongs to his life, completes him. As a final shot, Ida says: 'You're a Good Girl, Rose. You don't want anything to do with Him.' This is true in the sense Ida means it, and also, because of the capitals, in the sense (not intended by Ida, but there) that spiritually Rose is a blessed, saint-like person (made clear, with typical irony, at the moment she is beginning to sin) who shouldn't have anything to do with the Evil One—'Him', or Pinkie. A minute later, after Ida has blustered off, Pinkie says: 'You're a good girl, Rose.' Here the definition of good is something that suits him. And, as he feels it is necessary for his safety, he will marry her so that she will belong to him 'like a room or a chair'. This is a magnificent and searching moment. The brave and good one (having won a fight for someone else) gives herself entirely body and soul to the cowardly and evil one (having lost a fight for himself), puts herself in his power so unselfishly and trustingly that she does not sense his repulsion at the contact of their lips. As humble about herself as she is proud to belong to him, she swears never to let him down, never, never. Her face is 'blind lost': blind to his wickedness and her virtue; lost because she is deliberately sinning, beginning to be lost, damning herself, yet at the same time representing paradise lost, innocence and goodness lost by Pinkie long ago. No wonder that as he fetches up a smile for her it is 'uneasily, with obscure shame'.

The singular stirring of intimacy and tenderness in Pinkie does not last. Part Five shows him caught up again in Brighton and cabined, cribbed, confined by his vanities and fears. The absence of questions and suspicions at the inquest on Spicer and the dogged loyalty of Dallow fail to cheer him. He doesn't trust Cubitt now. No matter what he does he can never quite grasp safety. It is always a step away. The prayer, 'Dona nobis pacem', is unanswered. For his own good, all things must give way; a massacre may be necessary. Again the parallel with Macbeth is obvious.

Then there is the festering dread about the wedding and how one plays 'the game'. To learn, he goes out to the roadhouse in the '*real*' country ('they use their own eggs in the gin slings') and encounters Spicer's girl, Sylvie. She is the direct opposite to Rose, and belongs to nobody, unlike a room or a chair. She protests tearfully her undying regard for Spicer and understands now 'why people go into monasteries' (there is no little humour in this scene) but she is soon in heat and leading Pinkie across the car park, which was once a farmyard—and still is, with the beast-like coupling which is taking place. Her experience of this is deftly shown in her nice taste in cars: a Morris is no good, but she loves a Lancia. The 'hideous and commonplace act' has rarely been so exactly placed; it is worthy to stand with the typist scene in *The Waste Land*. It also reveals in vivid terms Pinkie's perversity. He will defy God and not flinch at damnation, but something that the despised Spicer could do with ease and gusto is impossible for him. Around him everyone is vigorous and skilled, a man diving in the 'pearly brilliant light', cleaving the water, and, again with the suggestion of love-making, two bathers swimming together, stroke by stroke, 'playing a private game, happy and at ease', in the world of right and wrong. But he with 'his narrow shoulders and hollow breast' is of another realm and can have fruitful union only with his complementary opposite—good.

Pinkie is tormented by two fears—of hanging and of 'the game'. After the failure with Sylvie, he protests that he would rather hang than marry. Then Rose, having been sacked for objecting to further pestering by Ida, enters with a newspaper with Spicer's picture, and wonders if she should go to the police. Her ingenuousness (which is like amazing shrewdness) is dangerous, and Pinkie wearily realizes that he must take this offered draught. Rose as he mused earlier when he and she were alone on top of the cliff might cease, the Law never. Again, ironically, he gets it wrong. What Rose represents—Love, Grace—is eternal and supersedes the Law, Goodness being stronger than Right, just as the New Testament supersedes the Old, as the blood of Christ on the cross supersedes the blood of sheep over the Israelites' lintels. Rose, sacrificing herself, prefers to go away with him unmarried, but agrees to a registrar's wedding, not because it makes the sin less but because it seems safer to Pinkie. Now he cannot avoid both her and hanging; he has to be arrested, and choosing the lesser evil he puts out his hands towards hers 'as if she were the detective with the cuffs'. (5, ii).

In the rest of Part Five, the typical juxtaposing of brief scenes, each balancing or contrasting with the others (like cinematic cross-cutting) is marked. Pinkie's visit to Rose's home shows pungently the horror from which he emerged, and the parents, Dickensian, 'treasuring their mood', sell their daughter. The evil and ugliness there are what Colleoni feeds on and are present in the Cosmopolitan with the thick luxury— a wedge of cream on Ida's plump tongue, hothouse

grapes and peaches, glacé shoes and jewelled pin, the
Pompadour Boudoir and the gaudy aphrodisiac
furnishings. Ida also 'treasures a mood'—for a bit of
fun—and, like Sylvie, abandons a man recently dead.
Back in Billy's, Pinkie (like most gang-leaders) faces a
challenge to his authority. Cubitt's sneers at Rose and
his gift of 'two little obscene objects' rasp Pinkie's most
raw sensibilities—his pride and his puritanism—and
fill him with such extraordinary indignation that he
violently threatens Cubitt and drives him away.
Cubitt's anger and suspicions are aroused, and he too
is ready to add to the various betrayals which are so
prominent in this part. And Ida, unsatisfied ('men
always failed you'), turns from the exhausted Phil to
her Mission, determined, ready to lend ear.

In Part Six Cubitt, paralleling Spicer in Part Three,
wanders about alone, filled, however, not with fear
but with what (this is a favourite point of Greene's)
may be more deadly—self-pity and sentimentality.
His appeal to Colleoni for a job and when this is
rejected his sloping even more fuddled to Ida echo
grotesquely the turning of an erring soul to God and
the Virgin Mother. He has 'an enormous urge to
confession' and he twice denies Pinkie, and a vague
memory of the Bible stirs Ida: 'a courtyard, a sewing
wench beside the fire, the cock crowing'. (6, i). She lies
too and learns about Spicer and how Hale was killed
but the unorthodoxy of this—'carving's different'
Cubitt reiterates maudlinly—sticks in his throat, the
recollection of the piece of Brighton Rock is so disturbing
that his fear takes over and Ida loses him. However,
she knows plenty and prepares with 'righteous mirth'
to save Rose from Pinkie.

This is exactly what Pinkie would do for himself, if he could. Outside the registrar's office, he waits with increasing nausea and terror, shaking as if with malaria. Things rank and gross possess him: the shops, the dog's ordure (earlier he thought marriage was like ordure on his hand), his memories of pornography and of the suicide of the fifteen-year-old Annie Collins, Drewitt's conventional suggestive witticisms and Dallow's facts about the pistils of flowers and the funny things they do. 'It's fun. It's the game', he declares, grinning with utter mirthlessness. And it should be stopped. Let us have no more marriages (his sex nausea resembles Hamlet's). He denies life: 'Credo in unum Satanam'. Just then Rose appears, representing the opposite principle, looking 'like one of the small gaudy statues in an ugly church'. (6, ii).

'God damn her', Pinkie cursed. She is coming to damn herself. And both know it. They are 'two Romans together in the grey street', moving out of the world of right and wrong into the realm of good and evil. It is a momentous act, quite the opposite of Ida's fun with Phil, and after this fall it will not be enough to smooth the hair with automatic hand and put a record on the gramophone. Pinkie is putting away childish things, his previous acts were trivial compared to this corruption. His pride persists: he watched Rose sign— 'his temporal safety in return for two immortalities of pain. He had no doubt whatever that this was mortal sin, and he was filled with a kind of gloomy hilarity and pride. He saw himself now as a full-grown man for whom the angels wept.' (6, ii). Most ironically, though, this self-congratulatory posture suggests that Pinkie is still immature, in a sense. He is sinning mortally and (unlike Ida) will burn, but this seems just a notion to him. If he felt it upon his pulses, if the truth were carried alive into his heart by passion, he would not be so smug. But he lacks imagination, and his pride is omnivorous.

The world is there—Drewitt with his stale jokes, Dallow with his clumsy kindness, the registrar, 'like a provincial actor' believing 'too much in his part' as if 'on the fringe of priestly office', and the whole disinfectant-smelling, lavatory-tiled plant and production line of official coupling, briskly supplied—'the market was firm'. Greene's contempt for 'state-made ceremony' (his prejudice against it, perhaps) has rarely been so biting and explicit.

The job done, the doors are locked and the bolt grinds into place, and Pinkie and Rose are 'shut out from an Eden of ignorance'. On this side of the grave there is 'nothing to look forward to but experience'. (6, ii). Like Adam and Eve, guilty and expelled after the Fall, Pinkie and Rose move about Brighton vainly seeking a home. Adam's curse is uttered and recorded for the future and his seed. Then they find themselves in the covered walk under the pier, the place of the first murder (paralleling Cain and Abel). The novel here is especially rich in meaning. It shows Pinkie's cleverness in selecting the one spot where nothing could be seen or heard of the killing of Hale in 'the noisiest, lowest, cheapest section of Brighton's amusements,' where 'the air was warm and thick and poisoned with human breath', a kind of Hades. There are two sorts of Brighton rock: the geological rock which surrounded the crime and in which it will be lodged for ever—like all our past actions (though the consequences of them

may be redeemed by God), and the confectionery rock
which stopped Hale's breath; pieces of the actual sticks
used, sold cheap, are sucked by Pinkie and Rose. This
represents an astounding parody of the act of com-
munion—holy and sexual (Pinkie is 'moved by a kind of
sensuality: the coupling of good and evil'): Rose with
her lips round the rock is taking the Devil into herself
(as she is soon to receive Pinkie carnally) just as Pinkie
in corrupting her is getting her and God in his guts:
'God couldn't escape the evil mouth which chose to
eat its own damnation.' (6, ii). Both are imbibing
damnation but with opposite intentions: she for love;
he for hatred. Typically, Pinkie longs to boast of his
own immense cleverness to 'relieve the enormous
pressure of pride'.

Because she loves him he is able to perform the
dreaded sexual act adequately. He exposes himself, but
no one laughs. He is not humbled, and an enormous
weight is lifted; he loses fear not vitality and he gains
'an invincible energy'. He has done everything, 'grad-
uated in the last human shame', succeeded in murder,
damnation and 'the game'. He is safely in Hell and it
is familiar. He has nothing to fear again, and is able to
listen to Cubitt's abuse with 'a kind of infernal pride';
he has 'outsoared the shadow of any night Cubitt
could be aware of', and he contemptuously dismisses
him.

His exhilaration is increased further when Rose
reveals that she knows he is a murderer and agrees
solemnly that she is as bad as he. But waking after the
nightmare, he again doubts her devotion. Hatred and
disgust are eternal, are always operating without our
effort. Love, though, makes demands, and he must

meet them if he is to continue to be safe; she has tied herself to him with love for here and hereafter even though it means damnation. Only death, he thinks, can set him free. Accordingly and very characteristically he preserves her message of love (the complete opposite of his on the record) to use against her.

Part Seven is the longest part. It is about twice as long as any of the other parts, except Part One which is about two-thirds of the size of Part Seven. In the first five sections Pinkie commits his greatest sin and error—mistrusting Rose and planning her death. Then, when all is safe, he finds he cannot face sixty years with her and he sets off the action leading to his end. The final two sections show Ida and Rose each confiding.

The morning after the wedding Rose also feels exhilarated and emancipated in the strange country of mortal sin. The act has changed her (she cannot agree with Judy, or with Ida, that it is just a bit of fun, not meaning anything at all). Now she has companions, she understands the relation between Dallow and Judy, and she has pride—Pinkie is affecting her. Compassion and honesty remain strong, however, and when she senses that her boasts about the joys of marriage are hurting Maisie, she avoids tempting her to sin and reveals that it is not all good. Faced though with Ida, unscrupulous and overbearing, she gives nothing away and, indomitable, once more rebuffs her. Yet Pinkie perversely turns this victory into defeat. Painfully he makes his 'appalling confession' that he trusts Dallow, but goes no further. He will not accept that Rose is true. She must be a polony and therefore treacherous. To believe otherwise would be to destroy his whole universe. She cleansed him with love, but now the empty tenement, his blank heart, is possessed by seven devils worse than the first. He seizes on the lie told by Rose to save him from anxiety, then when she confesses he assumes that this is a further instance of deceit. His is the cardinal sin of imputing evil motives; for him, 'No worst, there is none'. So, with tremendous irony, he is able to assure Rose (dazed and staggering as she realizes that he was also involved in the death of Spicer) that she can trust him. Under constant pressure from his pride and fear, with scope only for tactics and never strategy, he plots the ultimate horror.

His visit to Drewitt reveals a particularly vivid and noisome segment of Hell. Pinkie, although accustomed to some aspects of Hell, is fearfully fascinated by someone else's and by Drewitt's sufferings—he has never known anything like it; for the first time his imagination becomes active and he feels for another, perhaps because of Rose's influence. A notion and a creature are becoming real and personal. Drewitt, with his decayed public-school education, brings together echoes from plays dealing with damnable pride and ambition, *Macbeth* and *Dr. Faustus*, and with sexual morbidity, *Hamlet*, which add resonance to the novel. Drewitt's wife also is placed, the old mole bitter in her cave, with passion only for tinned salmon. Images of radical internal disease are marked in *Hamlet*, and Drewitt has his ulcer (both physical and spiritual) but he will not face the clean and severe cut which might cure him—he 'doesn't believe in the knife'. In his befuddled maudlin condition, wracked with pain and fear he confesses and Pinkie is in the position of a priest. But because there is no true religious element the confession is vain. Instead of humbling Drewitt and pointing him to penance and grace, it feeds his self-pity and pride, he is 'shaken by an enormous windy self-esteem', (7, iii), and it leads to his abandonment of his responsibilities and his flight to France.

Returning to Billy's, ready to relax in his cosy Hell, Pinkie finds it changed—it has been tidied up and she, his enemy, is there. He manages to control his anger, but it is clear that she must die. With her tied to him there is no refuge anywhere. She has sworn (it is there on the slip of paper in his pocket) that wherever he goes she will go too, and this she means simply and absolutely. And further, the horrible idea appears: she may have a child, 'the rivet of another life pinning him down' (7, iv) (the line stretching out to the crack of doom). She must go before her persistent love disperses all that he holds on to as real and true. Evil cannot endure the naked daily encounter with love. At her touch vice may go out of him like virtue, her warmth may thaw the icy confines of his Hell, he may no longer be himself, entire and self-absorbed. In the face of this threat everything else fades, the memories of Hale and Spicer become remote and muddled, the offer of peace (a good one, Dallow declares) from Colleoni is ignored—plainly it is 'all now him and her'.

This holds true even when it transpires that Drewitt has reached France and Cubitt will not inform and they are accordingly safe. Ida is still there, singing confidently, hanging on like a ferret, but looking across the pier restaurant to her Pinkie knows that '*this* hare escaped. He had no cause to fear her now'. Yet he is dull and apprehensive and will not celebrate with Dallow and Judy. Well-meaning as usual Dallow tries to cheer him up with the hope that he may live to

eighty with his missus. This focuses the horror for
Pinkie. He knows he cannot face sixty years with Rose.
Ida's laughter is like defeat for him, though she does not
know how. Thus with magnificent irony Pinkie is
hounded to doom not only by Ida, not only by the
world of right and wrong, but by his complementary
opposite, Rose. Or rather by his fear of the one force,
the only being in the universe, that has a genuine
concern for him and longs to save him. He flies from
love, not hate. Plausibly he lies, using the fact of Ida's
relentless pursuit to persuade Rose that there is no
alternative to suicide and prepares for the inquest on
her by planting clues before setting out for Peacehaven,
aptly chosen, where he trusts his prayer for peace will
be answered. It is, but not in the way he anticipates. He
intends that she should shoot herself first and then he
would break his promise immediately to kill himself.
At the inquest the slip of paper would serve as evidence
of suicidal intentions by Rose and little blame would
attach to him.

As they drive along there is intense activity, mental
and spiritual. This is the climax of the novel and it
involves a superbly articulated reversal of values and
belief which, paradoxically, affirms what Pinkie and
Rose are denying—for opposite reasons. Rose puts
Pinkie before God and shows her love by resisting God.
She regards all the good impulses of her Catholic
training as bad, and the suggestions from Pinkie as
good. Sin is Behovely, and the greater the sin against
God, the greater her virtue and her love for Pinkie.
It is Pinkie not God she trusts, and the orthodox evil
act becomes the good one, the betrayal of God the only
loyal deed. Similarly, Pinkie is steadfast to evil, as a

saint is steadfast to God. His temptation is to heed the pleas or warnings of God; his sin would be to feel remorse or love, his treachery to save Rose.

Going through the dark Pinkie speaks feelingly of the horrors of life—'worms and cataract, cancer'—and she has insufficient experience of joy to contradict him firmly. When she realizes that he is determined to die and be damned she prepares to follow suit. She would 'show Them that They couldn't damn him without damning her too'; he seemed like a child to her, and 'she felt responsibility move in her breasts; she wouldn't let him go into that darkness alone'. (7, vii). For his part he is anxious to accept her sacrifice; it will make all plain and easy: 'Life would go on. No more human contacts, other people's emotions washing at the brain—he would be free again: nothing to think about but himself. Myself'. Unable to conceive of Heaven, trusting in Hell, Pinkie has nevertheless a moment of awful resentment against Heaven that he has been condemned by squalor from his birth and never been given a glimpse of Heaven through a crack between the hideous Brighton walls. As he thinks this, he takes a long look at Rose. He fails to see that there is no cause for his resentment; something of Heaven is alive by his side. The Hound of Heaven does not give up. He stirs Pinkie through tenderness, a 'prowling pressure of pity'.

They go in a pub for Rose to write her suicide message and there enter two upper-class lechers, with their sports car, camel-hair coats and beer from tankards, speaking of humans like machines and machines like humans and certain that everything has a price—apt representatives of the world of right and wrong, and

quite oblivious of the eternal drama going on round
them. They arrogantly dismiss Rose as being unworthy
of their attentions, and angry at this, Pinkie feels for
her—tenderness looks in at the window. He has a sudden
inclination to throw up the whole thing. He gives Rose
one more chance, asking her if she will love him always.
She says she will and dooms herself. If there were a
chance of her being unfaithful and leaving him, he
might not need her death, but her constancy forces
him wearily on. Still God will not let him be. In this
extremity between stirrup and ground grace is offered.
God tries desperately to get in to him, as Pinkie is
touched by his memories of the marriage night:

> There had been a kind of pleasure, a kind of pride,
> a kind of—something else . . . An enormous emotion
> beat on him; it was like something trying to get in,
> the pressure of gigantic wings against the glass. (7, ix).

He resists it with concentrated hatred and fear bred
from the pain and treachery and squalor he has
experienced all his life. If 'the beast' got in there would
be a 'huge havoc' and he would be transformed. It is
God still pursuing, offering the peace for which he
prays; but the price—'the confession, the penance, and
the sacrament'—is too much. He will not serve. The
parallel between Pinkie and Satan is close here. As
he pretends to take farewell of the world he thinks
with supreme blasphemy of the last gospel (from St.
John) in the Mass: 'He was in the world and the world
was made by Him and the world knew Him not', and
he puts himself in the place of Christ. Just as Christ
was not recognized by the world, so he, for quite
opposite reasons, has not been recognized. His hatred

is god-like: he would do such things . . . but he has not been given a chance. The contrast is most telling between the enormity of his ambition and the slightness of his achievements, between his boundless pride and his immature figure, full of self-pity because no one appreciates him.

Rose loves him, however; with that greater love that will lay down life, even eternal life, for a friend. This most amazing and palpable and redeeming truth he ignores as she prepares to shoot herself, and he brushes her cheek with his Judas kiss. It is a bizarre Gethsemane. Just in time the rescuers and captors arrive; and the ironic association with Christ is made. The princes of this world, not knowing what they do, act and produce good: Christ's crucifixion provides redemption for mankind, and Pinkie is dispatched steaming and in appalling agony (as if the flames of Hell had literally got him) to nothing. And Rose is saved, ironically enough, by Ida from whom she has constantly fled. It is good for Rose that here she is, for the only time, defeated by Ida. Even the world of right and wrong would seem to have its uses. Maybe there is a Providence at work (Pinkie was withdrawn as if by a hand) comprehending everything;

> And all shall be well and
> All manner of thing shall be well
> When the tongues of flame are in-folded
> Into the crowned knot of fire
> And the fire and the rose are one.
>
> (T. S. Eliot, *Four Quartets*)

Certainly Ida thinks all has turned out well. She is 'like a figurehead of Victory' in the pub as she explains things to Clarence. He puts one or two fairly shrewd questions but he is mainly a feed for her and his judgement that she is 'a terrible woman' is favourable. She acted for the best. Ida, agreeing, adds that she knows what Love is (Rose will vehemently contradict this) and modestly gives the credit to a higher power: the Board saved Rose. The ludicrous yet dangerous complacency of this travesty of confession and judgement is underlined by the contrast with the real confession of Rose. Unlike the gaudy Ida, the priest and the believers are unattractive and dingy (as is usual in Greene), and Rose does not interpret circumstances to suit herself. She believes, as she has been taught, that Pinkie is damned. The story of Péguy (7, xi) astounds her but she is too humble to see its significance for herself, and the priest's admission that no one can conceive 'the appalling . . . strangeness of the mercy of God' does not move her much. Then he suggests that if Pinkie loved her at all, even if only 'love like that' (merely physical), there is perhaps hope, especially 'if there's a baby'. This is it, the hope, the prospect of release from the worst horror, the complete circle— being back at home, at Snow's, as if Pinkie had never existed. With a child, the product of their love, she could go on living, reminding 'them' from generation to generation of Pinkie. But, and this is the final and terrible (and necessary) twist of the knife, the record will soon declare that he didn't love her at all, not even 'like that'. That hope spoken of by the priest will prove to be vain, though not perhaps all hopes. There is still the child, and her faith, the enduring strength of which is indicated by her present suffering. She is for the dark night. Yet it is Love which devised the torment, 'wove the intolerable shirt of flame', and teaches us

... to sit still

Even among these rocks,
Our peace in His will.

(T. S. Eliot, *Ash Wednesday*)

Questions

1. Specify what qualities you appreciate in the opening of a novel.

2. Consider the point of having seven parts to *Brighton Rock*. Calculate how much space is devoted to each part, and compare the amounts. Indicate if there is any particular theme or quality in each part and give each a descriptive title.

3. Show how Greene increases the speed of his narration as he approaches a climax.

4. Collect instances of irony and deliberate ambiguity and show their uses.

5. Evaluate the evidence for and against the proposition that the murder of Hale is the first murder committed by the gang.

6. State precisely where Pinkie made mistakes and suggest how he might have avoided them.

7. Imagine that Dallow and Drewitt are having a drink together on the night of the wedding of Rose and Pinkie and write a dialogue between them.

8. Arrange trials for the murders of Hale and/or Spicer. Take parts appropriately, bringing in various characters as accused, defence, prosecution, witnesses, judge, jury, reporters, and television commentators.

9. What considerations would you bear in mind in assessing a novel?

CHARACTERS and SETTING

The basic conflict between the world of right and wrong and the realm of good and evil is seen in the moving pattern of the characters, in their natures and functions and in their appearances. Ida and Colleoni are fleshly and materially powerful, while Pinkie and Rose are physically slight. With the 'soft chicken down' on his face, the 'slight tic', his narrow shoulders and the shabby suit too thin from wear, the pointed shoes which have 'never walked farther than the length of the parade', his lack of skills (he has never used his razor on an armed enemy) and his ineptitude in love-making, he is not remarkable. Unless you notice his face, its 'starved intensity, a kind of hideous and unnatural pride' and especially his eyes, slaty grey, 'like those of an old man in whom human feeling has died'. (1, i). This is the point, and it is made several times, that he is literally as proud as the devil.

What shaped him? His environment, to a large extent. 'Man is made by the places in which he lives.' 'Hell lay about him in his infancy' in the ugliness and brutality of Paradise Piece (aptly echoing the Garden and the Fall). Nobody could say, he declares fiercely, sensing again its horror as he visits Rose's home, that 'he hadn't done right to get away from this, to commit any crime'. (5, iii). This environment and the attempts to escape it have made him what he is—physically a weakling but strong in will and with imagination inert, completely self-centred and pitiless; one with infinite desires, twisted and outrageous, and with the belief that he could attain them only by cunning, cruelty and betrayal. He was helped by a substitute father, the

71

only person he liked—Kite, and on Kite's death he inherited his mannerisms, 'the bitten thumb-nail, the soft drinks' and the duty of never leaving the territory and of avenging him. He is a quick and ingenious liar and as a gang leader he shows resolution and resource, craft and daring, but he is hampered by his lack of experience and under remorseless pressure is unable to control events long enough for strategy, only for tactics. Also constantly operating is the loss of innocence, the curse of his childhood, which has made him a sadist. The sexual exercise of his parents each Saturday night, his father panting 'like a man at the end of a race', and his mother making horrifying sounds of pleasurable pain, filled him with lasting nausea and revulsion. He is never more vocal than when describing this, and Dallow is astonished at the 'sudden horrified gift of tongues'. (6, ii). This experience perverted him and gave him a radical loathing of sex. For him it is not natural, not a bit of fun (as it is for Ida and Dallow) but it is 'a dirty scramble' 'worth murdering a world' to avoid. Sex is a sickness, or like 'a file on metal or the touch of velvet to a sore hand'. At a mention of it or of bodily functions where 'love has pitched his mansion' his intense prudishness is offended, his virginity ('bitter, soured, cruel') 'straightens like sex'. To escape it he swore as a child to become a priest, and there is something of the spoiled priest about him (ironically Rose goes to him for guidance) and he might conduct a Black Mass. (Herbert Haber in a clever article: 'The Two Worlds of Graham Greene' in *Modern Fiction Studies*, *III*, Autumn 1957, pp. 256–68, suggests that the novel may be seen as the inversion of the seven sacraments, each of which Pinkie dishonours.)

Pinkie's sadism is marked, the expression of his sexual energies: cruelty straightens his body like lust, the finest of all sensations is the infliction of pain. It is often associated with sentimental music which moans in his head, wails, grief in his guts, which is the nearest he knows to sorrow, just as the 'faint sensual pleasure' he feels as he touches the bottle of vitriol with his fingers is 'his nearest approach to passion'. (2, i). Aldous Huxley in *Antic Hay* speaks of the amazing potency of cheap music and this certainly applies to Pinkie. Occasionally it is merged with the music he remembers from his choir-boy days, as in his joy at the end of Part Three when he believes he has fixed Spicer's death. Generally the church music is overshadowed by the jazz which has become in Pinkie's tortured mind almost a substitute for religious emotion (as, in a less unhealthy way, it has become almost a substitute for great national ceremonies for the crowds at the dance —in Part Two, section one.) After his marriage Pinkie seeing a romantic musical film is overwhelmed 'in a wash of incredible moonshine', and weeps and longs to repent and find peace. But it is bogus, self-indulgent, an indication of his chaotic values. When causing suffering, physical or mental, he is callous and assured, hence he cannot experience contrition merely through the jazz: 'the ribs of his body were like steel bands which held him down to eternal unrepentance'. (6, ii). Similarly, at the dance, he sings softly 'in his spoilt boy's voice: "Agnus Dei qui tollis peccata mundi, dona nobis pacem." In his voice a whole lost world moved; the lighter corner below the organ, the smell of incense and laundered surplices, and the music . . . any music moved him, speaking of things he didn't understand.' (2, i).

This is a pointer to the fact that although Pinkie's background and upbringing explain a great deal about him they don't explain everything. Modern psychology and sociology demonstrate (what people had a pretty shrewd notion about already) that bad environment and training can permanently corrupt or impair an individual. Greene shows an understanding of this and reveals a kinship with other young writers of the Thirties who felt that such understanding and vast changes in society were necessary to make life better for individuals. But, Greene affirms, political, economic, sociological and psychological factors do not entirely determine a person's character and career (Rose and Piker exposed to the same influences as Pinkie turn out differently from him). There are other forces at work entwined with the factors mentioned above, and these forces can be decisive. Pinkie has been brought into touch with them through Catholicism, and although he rejects it, it persists and enables him to place the world he knows. This world, so squalid and brutal is clearly an expression of Hell, and anyone who refuses to believe in Hell, he fiercely declares, is ignoring the appalling evidence for it all around. Thus Pinkie's upbringing and the Church's teaching have taken him beyond the world of right and wrong and given him a spiritual insight which nearly all the other characters lack. It is one familiar in Greene's fiction—the rejection of the comfortable illusion that this world can ever be fully happy and satisfying and the awareness of the reality of sin and evil and of their counterparts, grace and goodness. Unfortunately Pinkie stops at the first part of the proposition; his insight is partial and black. He sees the evil all right, but although the Church teaches also of love and Heaven, he will have none of them. Heaven is just a notion, he has not felt it on his pulses, as he has felt Hell:

> Heaven was a word; Hell was something he could trust. A brain was capable of only what it could conceive, and it couldn't conceive what it had never experienced; his cells were formed of the cement school playground, the dead fire and the dying man in the St. Pancras waiting-room, his bed at Billy's and his parents' bed. An awful resentment stirred in him—why shouldn't he have had his chance like all the rest, seen his glimpse of Heaven if it was only a crack between the Brighton walls? (7, vii).

There is truth in this; he has been deprived and handicapped by his terrible upbringing and environment, and he has had few opportunities to experience anything but ugliness and pain; but there was a radical change in his circumstances when he became involved with Rose. She represents and offers the other part of the whole, the goodness, the glimpse of Heaven, and it is ironic that at the very instant of his feeling the appalling resentment, she is at his side ready to damn herself for him, and the grace of God is desperately trying to get to him. Sometimes he senses a kinship with her. At the end of their first meeting he says with contemptuous sarcasm (which she does not notice) that they have things in common. He intends merely to use her for his own safety but as he becomes involved her fidelity touches him like cheap music. She defends him against Ida, and he feels no antagonism but a faint nostalgia (for his fall and lost innocence). He and Rose inhabit a realm which is foreign to Ida and the rest: 'he was aware that she belonged to his life, like a room or a chair: she was something which completed him, . . . What was most evil in him needed her: it couldn't get along without goodness . . . She was good, he'd discovered that, and he was damned; they were made for each other.' (4, iii). And again at times during the wedding and after he feels companionship in her goodness and a sense that she completes him. Through her love he is able to perform the sex act adequately and overcome his fear of 'the game.' But these are moments only, intuitions, glimpses of Heaven, and he does not will them to last. He will not make the surrender of self and accept the good, the solution, which she and God continually offer. He rejects the service which leads to perfect freedom. Non serviam, he cries with his lord, 'credo in unum Satanam'. The deadliest of sins, that which sent the once glorious Archangel and Man falling, is paramount. Pride is present immediately on Pinkie's first appearance and it prevails throughout. Even after it has been cleared for a time through intercourse with Rose, it returns seven times worse. It is insatiable. Because of this and partly because of his strange feelings about Rose there develops a longing for peace. To gain this peace, to feed his pride, to assert his individual self, come what may, he is prepared (like Macbeth), to do anything, to carve the whole bloody boiling, to massacre the world. But all his energies go astray and make confusion worse confounded. He is a tormented creature, seeking safety and redemption in the wrong way, ignoring the support and grace offered through Rose and destroying himself both in worldly and metaphysical terms. He would reject everyone; a 'dim desire for annihilation' stretches in him, 'the vast superiority of vacancy' (5, iii); more and more he longs for 'no more human contacts, other people's emotions washing at the brain—he would be free again: nothing to think about but himself. Myself.' Hence the rest, the end, he attains is that always mirrored in his 'grey, inhuman, ageless' eyes, 'the annihilating eternity from which he had come and to which he went.' (1, ii).

It is a supreme irony that Rose who might have saved Pinkie from both material disaster and spiritual annihilation, had he heeded her, wishes for his sake to be damned herself. At first she seems hardly likely to rise to the height of this great argument.

With a background similar to Pinkie's, Rose is diffident and not striking physically. Pale and thin, with mousy hair flat on her small scalp, her face bony and her eyes too far apart, and with no dress sense, she will never make a stir in this world. Her conversation is devoid of Ida's soiled experience and Pinkie's enormous ambitions. She is also different from Pinkie in her attitude to her environment. Although she loathes the filth of her home, she endures her lot, while Pinkie rebels against it. Both are convincing: in material terms, she a poor girl has had little opportunity of knowing better, while he a deprived youth drawn into crime has glimpsed (not Heaven) but power and wealth through Kite and Colleoni; in spiritual terms, she has patience and hope while he having rejected the source of these and other virtues is possessed by envy, greed and pride.

She accepts gratefully and almost pathetically what little she has: the 'good job' at Snow's among the paper napkins and the sauce bottles, the trip to the scarred and shabby country, the ice-cream, the rock and the record with the frightful message. Yet she is not a fool. She quickly senses that something is wrong, she recognizes Spicer's voice on the telephone and his photograph, and although she is naturally warm and agreeable with Ida at first, she closes up immediately she spots danger for Pinkie. In fact, although in appearance unremarkable, she has more of certain kinds of maturity and strength than anyone else in the story. These come partly from her innocence—her better natural instincts have not been corrupted by self-indulgence as Ida's have nor by ambition as Pinkie's have—and mainly from her faith. Her fresh maternal feelings are very strong, she will fight, tooth and nail, to save Pinkie. She has tenderness and passion in sex and she conceives a child to whom she will be devoted—quite the opposite to Ida, Sylvie and Judy, for whom sex is sterile fleshly play.

Rose's faith encourages mental clarity. Logically she knows that by the teachings of the Church she and Pinkie are in mortal sin. She watches people returning from Mass: she 'didn't envy them and she didn't despise them; they had their salvation and she had Pinkie and damnation.' She rejects evasion or deception and does not, unlike Ida with her ouija board, expect Divine powers to proclaim what best suits her desires. She too believes in Justice and is prepared to accept its verdict. Molly Carthew despaired and killed herself and is in Hell; and Rose allows that such a punishment is meet for her too. That the cause of the sin was wholly love, she does not take into account, though from what the old priest says, God well may. Knowing that she has freely willed her damnation, and severe upon herself, she is reluctant to accept the comfort of the old priest about the appalling strangeness of the mercy of God. Humble, she does not feel worthy of it, and her resolve to go on living comes from love not doctrine, love for Pinkie still and for her unborn child. It is typical of the paradox which runs through the novel that her love, a reflection of Divine Love surely, is at its greatest when she is absolutely defying God and giving herself absolutely to the Devil. This is precisely what Pinkie does. But it is the motive (which only God fully knows) which marks the difference. Pinkie does it entirely for his own sake. She does it entirely for him. 'Greater love hath no man than this' she falteringly recites (7, i) and quite without regard to herself she has this love and wills to lay down her immortal life for her friend. There is then not only something of the saint and martyr but also, as her name suggests, something of the Blessed Virgin Mother of God, of Christ himself even, in her. She thus embodies the main positive values in the novel, and is the one to withstand Ida. The conflicts between these two are at the heart of the novel, defining its basic stress and pattern and the essential natures and relationships of Rose, Pinkie and Ida.

Rose is kind with people she meets and she criticizes no one (except Ida) but she is presented in noteworthy contact only with Pinkie and Ida (though, of course, along with this, she has a relationship with God). Once her love has been engaged for Pinkie she identifies herself completely with him and completely against Ida. From the first she insists that Ida is different from Pinkie and her, and she gives a reason for it: Ida has no distress, no care or trust for anything beyond

herself, you 'can tell the world's all dandy with her.'
What Pinkie and Rose do has significance, even Rose's
presumably very normal and absolved mortal sin at
the age of twelve, but Ida feeling no despair and no
need to atone is stunted and ignorant with her
obsession with right and wrong. No matter what Pinkie
has done, Rose would rather burn with him than be like
her. The crucial confrontation comes after Ida,
fortified with winnings from Black Boy, 'an infinite
capacity for corruption,' goes, like a warship, into
action. Primed with an appetite to do good, she will
save Rose, come what may. But her patience, 'almost
as deep as her good will', is soon exhausted. With
plump and patronizing paw' raised for a blow, she barks
that Rose is morbid—the customary label for one who
voluntarily maintains a position which involves suffering
oneself—and sneers that Rose is innocent. So she is—
innocent of Ida's world. But so too is Ida innocent of
Rose's realm, though Rose is not able to say how:

> 'You're young. That's what it is,' Ida said, 'romantic.
> I was like you once. You'll grow out of it. All you
> need is a bit of experience.' The Nelson Place eyes
> stared back at her without understanding; driven to
> her hole the small animal peered out at the bright
> and breezy world: in the hole were murder, copu-
> lation, extreme poverty, fidelity, and the love and
> fear of God; but the small animal had not the
> knowledge to deny that only in the glare and open
> world outside was something which people called
> experience. (4, ii).

Rose is here instinctively upholding realities far
deeper than the rational. Ida is out of touch with them,

'in a strange country: the typical Englishwoman abroad. She hadn't even got a phrase book.' She is as far from Rose and Pinkie as she is 'from Hell—or Heaven. Good and evil lived in the same country, spoke the same language, came together like old friends'. Ida is ignorant. Blundering, she tries flattery, but receives again the same reply: 'You don't know a thing.' Defeated, she retreats blustering and threatening. There is the same result to the final battle. Again she tries cajolery and threats, thinking to shock Rose by the disclosure that Pinkie is a murderer; but it is she who is shocked when Rose quietly says she knows and it doesn't matter; Ida's 'good-natured, ageing face' stares 'like an idiot's from the ruins of a bombed home'. Rose following up adroitly gets some useful information out of her, ignores her warnings and threats and challenges her view that human nature, like Brighton rock, never changes, is the same all the way down: '"Confession . . . repentance," Rose whispered.' Then realizing that so long as she is bound in mortal sin to Pinkie confession and repentance are not for them, she is disconcerted, and Ida, crying, 'That's just religion,' comes back fiercely, but Rose recovers, and the inhumanity beneath Ida's fun-loving, easy nature is exposed on the rock of Rose's unflinching gaze: '"Obstinate," Ida said. "If I was your mother . . . a good hiding." The bony and determined face stared back at her; all the fight there was in the world lay there—warships cleared for action and bombing fleets took flight—between the set eyes and the stubborn mouth'. (7, i). While Ida emits her worldly wisdom and admonishments, the aphorisms 'clicking out like a ticket from a slot machine', Rose, quite untouched, broods darkly: 'a God wept in a garden and cried out upon a cross: Molly Carthew went to everlasting fire.' Finally, infuriated, Ida flings out mercilessly the sarcastic caution against becoming pregnant with a murderer's baby, and again the result is the opposite of what she anticipated. Rose is filled with a sense of glory and hope for the future. And Ida is defeated. She tries a come-back after the death of Pinkie and officiously takes Rose to her parents, but to no avail. Rose's verdict in the confessional is indisputable: 'She doesn't know about love.' (7, xi).

Rose does. Without being fully aware of it and without being able to articulate it, she embodies love, secular and divine, and is, perhaps more than Pinkie, the central character in the novel. It depends on her: 'the still point of the turning world', though hidden, and, like the Word made flesh, unrecognized by many. There are two vital distinctions to be made, and Rose makes them both. The distinction between the world of right and wrong and the realm of good and evil, and the distinction between good and evil. In the world of right and wrong (inhabited by Ida and nearly all the others), there is a difference between right and wrong, Ida insists, but, as Rose makes clear, there is no need to bother about it; the two words, right and wrong meant nothing to Rose. 'Their taste was extinguished by stronger foods—Good and Evil. The woman could tell her nothing she didn't know about these—she knew by tests as clear as mathematics that Pinkie was evil—what did it matter in that case whether he was right or wrong?' (7, i). There is, though, a basic difference within the realm of good and evil (inhabited by Rose and Pinkie and incidentally by the old priest

and the derelict old woman with 'rotting and dis-
coloured face' that Pinkie, horrified, sees after his
marriage). And it is Rose again paradoxically while
trying to identify herself completely with Pinkie who
makes this clear. Pinkie says to her: '"You don't want
to listen too much to priests. They don't know the
world like I do. Ideas change, the world moves on . . ."
His words stumbled before her carved devotion. That
face said as clearly as words that ideas never changed,
the world never moved: it lay there always the ravaged
and disputed territory between the two eternities.
They faced each other as it were from opposing
territories, but like troops at Christmas-time they
fraternized.' (5, ii). Thus Rose shows that although
good and evil need and complete each other (in a
reality which both includes and transcends the world
of right and wrong), there is an enduring hostility
between them. She also, despite herself in a way,
testifies powerfully to the wonder and ultimate
superiority of love and good.

There is another paradox: the rotting and dis-
coloured derelict saying her prayers resembles Ida
Arnold—her body is like Ida's mind; her spirit is like
Ida's body, in pretty good shape. In terms of
recognizable images from everyday life, Ida is the
most vividly presented character. This is natural; she
is so much of the world that hosts of images from it
are appropriate (though it takes someone of Greene's
quality to select them). For Pinkie and Rose, though,
having relations with the realm of good and evil,
images and allusions from the religious life are also
used.

The carnal glow of Ida is marked from the first; her

magnificent breasts and legs, her laughter and songs and her rich Guinness voice; she is matey, one of the decent, cheery, homely folk, knowing what's what, having fun, coy and provocative, finding the world all dandy, great, so long as you don't weaken. Smelling of soap and wine, with her breasts and thighs and big tipsy mouth, she suggests mother and the nursery, and exudes a slow sleepy physical enjoyment, comfort and peace. (1, i). No wonder that Pinkie with his starved intensity and belief in Hell hates her instantly (though, later, they unite, in a way, against Rose) and that many men, like Hale, are drawn and long to lose themselves in her. A representative of good mother earth, a fertility symbol, one might think, but, in fact, not so. She is sterile and phoney and very dangerous. She has no children, and though she may have lots of easy acquaintances her men friends are feeble. There is far more show than substance. In the aphrodisiac fake Pompadour Boudoir, she takes the éclair between her lips, squeezing it with her plump tongue and enjoying the spurt of rich cream, but a bit later with the actualities of sex she is unsatisfied and Phil is exhausted and apprehensive: 'She might just as well have been to the pictures.' Much with her is substitute: she bears 'the same relation to passion as a peep-show' (5, iv), much is stereotype or second-hand, on the surface. Inside there is emptiness and loneliness, but she does not recognize it, she is adept at avoiding any unpleasant facts, she can never think of herself as dead; death is too shocking, life is so important, and life is 'sunlight on brass bedposts, ruby port, the leap of the heart when the outsider you have backed passes the post,' Fred's lips pressing down in the taxi vibrating along the parade. This life is all there is and therefore anyone who takes life must be punished. Ida is ready to play God—like other characters in Greene's fiction, though Rowe in *The Ministry of Fear* and Scobie in *The Heart of the Matter* act from motives quite different from Ida's. She, with enormous presumption, adopts the role of the God of the Old Testament and proclaims that vengeance is hers. She pursues it remorselessly. A sticker, 'barnacled with pieces of popular wisdom', carrying 'her air of compassion and comprehension about her like a rank perfume' (7, viii), 'her big breasts ready for any secrets', she goes after vengeance with daring and strength, using her wide experience of the soiled world to deceive, to flatter, to bully and to destroy.

From the moment of her dedication to avenging Hale, she is associated with images of warfare. The over-ripe charm and the pitiless belligerency are united. Ida is a striking representative of that prevalent and dangerous mixture (which Greene rightly censures) of sentimentality and callousness which is often consequent upon atrophy of the imagination. Squeezing out tears into a handkerchief scented with Californian Poppy for poor Fred or softening at the notion of a romantic return to Tom, she is typically moved by facile nostalgia, by the objects of her 'good life' stored in the glass-fronted cupboard; shallow pathos easily touches 'her friendly and popular heart'. Mushy and indulgent with herself, she is mawkish and agreeable with others so long as she gets her own way. But when she is opposed or threatened she becomes aggressive and hard. Her feelings are so raw and badly nourished and uneducated that she cannot project them outside herself really to feel for anyone else or to imagine the consequences of her actions. She loses any memory of Hale and becomes quite irresponsible, pressing on in sheer self-assertion, hooking on smiles as you hook on a wreath, demanding Justice 'as if she were ordering a pound of tea'. It is a ghastly parody of a Holy War, her mission to proclaim the difference between right and wrong, to make someone suffer; and, yet, after all, it is fun, exciting, a bit of life. She goes on, confirming that the world is a good place, if you don't weaken, 'like a chariot in a triumph' with 'all the big battalions behind her' and at the end she stands 'like a figurehead of Victory', certain that she understands love, her job well done, and like a good and faithful servant rendering all praise and thanks to—the Board.

The other characters necessarily are not so fully developed, some are properly flat not round, yet all have recognizable human characteristics. The gangsters are driven by greed, fear, and pride, each in different proportions. Hale, with his inky fingers and bitten nails, is increasingly scared but maintains his pride in his superior experience and position almost to the end. In Spicer fear quickly predominates and after some hope on the race-course he is extinguished. Cubitt, more thick-skinned, is untroubled for a time and follows his appetites. Coarse and vulgar he chafes Pinkie's rawest point then lacking the spirit to sustain his rebellion he goes off feeling unappreciated and confides in Ida. But her offer of twenty pounds rouses his fear more than his greed and he clears out. Dallow, devoted and dumb, has less mental life than any of them (the contrast between his reaction to Spicer's murder and Drewitt's is instructive). He is the sturdy muscle-man, living seemingly at a level below the moral; near the end his face is twice described as 'broad, brutal and innocent'. (7, v). For him 'the world's all right if you don't go too far'. Faithful and roughly affectionate himself and with a kind of tolerance he senses something of Rose's virtues. Killing her would be going too far, and he warns Pinkie that he will not stand for it. And it is his desire to warn Pinkie that leads with the quick-witted assistance of Ida to the rescue of Rose. These men are generally losers. They have vices enough, but they are not able to exploit them with the wholesale determination, craft and strength of the successful gangsters. Colleoni, the boss, is what Pinkie would be. Colleoni, however, seems to exist at only one level, and in this and other ways he is akin to Ida. He has certainly done well: 'he looked as a man might look who owned the whole world, the whole visible world, that is: the cash registers and policemen and prostitutes, Parliament and the laws which say "this is Right and this is Wrong".' (2, ii). He is a business man, Colleoni affirms four times, as if this justifies any conduct however underhand or vicious; he is successful and respectable, and may well be going in for politics: 'the Conservatives think a lot of him'. Snug and protected in the 'huge moneyed hotel' he is at home; he has not been on a race-course for twenty years. His world and Pinkie's do not touch, he says. This is true in one sense (though his lush existence is dependent on the same sources and he has not the excuse that a deprived youth of seventeen might have for persisting in evil), but it is true also in a profounder sense which he is ignorant of for he feels no distress or need for forgiveness and he could not burn. He talks in patronizing business jargon: he likes push, 'the world needs young people with energy'. One who patently has these qualities is Crab. With his dyed hair and straightened nose, 'in a mauve suit with shoulders like coat hangers and a small waist', he has got on (unlike Spicer and Cubitt) and is 'part of the great racket.' He flaunts himself before them and in an interview with Cubitt (which neatly parallels Colleoni's with Pinkie), he flourishes his cigar and gold lighter and patronizingly and insultingly warns Cubitt off. Greed and envy and conceit are pervasive. And so are other appetites. These are grossly indulged in with Sylvie and Judy, molls and wantons both yet sufficiently differentiated, who not only provide a conventional carnal element, but also enable certain qualities in Rose and Pinkie to be revealed.

Ida's male companions are much less lusty and able and are comparatively elderly. She is sorry for Charlie Moyne, 'a poor old geezer, in a check coat, a yellow waistcoat, and a grey bowler, with a sidelong raffish look and a jaunty and ancient despair'. Clarence she calls an old ghost, a 'sombre thin man in black with a bowler hat', and her main attendant, Phil Corkery, looks as if he needs feeding up, as if he is 'wasted with passions he has never had the courage to pursue far enough' (3, i) and after undertaking Ida he lies 'yellow with sexual effort', exhausted and apprehensive. This is rather surprising. Surely a woman so easy and voluptuous as Ida would have more virile and present-able admirers? Or is it again being suggested that Ida is more show than substance, that her sensuality and ample charms are fake and arid? This can hardly be the case as these are insisted on and she has to be genuinely carnal for her place in the pattern and to be a worthy opposite to Rose. It may be that only the fading men of Ida's acquaintance are presented to indicate what she may be like in fifteen years time and so that they can act as foils to her. She proudly explains and justifies herself to them and they seem like confessors, though, unlike priests—and this is a point—they are dominated by her and are in no position to give guidance.

There are some characters who do not fall into any group. Drewitt, for instance. He, like Charlie Moyne though more fully and deeply, is a characteristic and penetrating Greene portrait of decayed gentility. Unlike the others he has had talent, education and prospects, and he understands and feels what he has lost and how degraded are his life and surroundings; beneath the spry appearance, the pat jokes and the tricky moves is despair; he is tormented both physically and mentally, he is in hell and he knows it. This uniquely moves and appals Pinkie. In Drewitt Pinkie for the first time recognizes and makes contact with a suffering creature, one of the damned, apparently. Opposite to Drewitt is one of the saved, presumably, Piker. He and Pinkie are 'oddly alike and allusively different' (7, vii) and they bristle 'like dogs at the sight of each other'. The introduction of this new character right at the end as Pinkie is attempting the ultimate sin, is a further instance of Greene's mastery. Piker (with similar upbringing and even name) a regular Catholic is what Pinkie might well have become had he not chosen ruthless self-assertion, just as Piker is the man Rose might well have married had she not sided with Pinkie (her good by his evil) to sacrifice herself entirely for love. A final contrast is between the true priest—the gentle old priest with a cold who helps Rose—and the pseudo priest, the bumptious registrar of marriages, and the unsavoury Old Crowe, guardian and manipulator of the Board.

Even the incidental characters have apt touches of individuality: Rose's parents treasuring their moods, Mrs. Drewitt with tousled hair, duster in hand, bitter and suspicious, watching visitors from her basement cave, and Molly Pink, fat and spotty, sucking toffee, making tea, reading *Woman and Beauty*, in awe of 'the partners' yet able to give Ida a clue. Then there are the bookies, Brewer and Tate, hollow and cheery, 'like a legend on a racing card', shifty and disreputable, reluctantly paying tribute to the gangsters; and other people in a position to see what is going on but not taking sides: the barmen, sources of information that may sometimes be tapped, and the shooting-booth attendant who doesn't want to be used in an alibi. Nearly all the characters are appropriately on the fringes of society and do no regular work. The authorities keep an eye on them, but the police play little part, preferring to let the lawless creatures devour themselves: the police inspector says to Pinkie: 'I don't mind you carving each other up in a quiet way. I don't give a penny for your worthless skins, but when two mobs start scrapping, people who matter may get hurt—decent, innocent people.' (2, ii).

But in a sense there are no innocent people. All really partake of their tainted setting. And writing which presents a corrupt and instinctive world, Greene felt, is nearer to enduring realities than writing which is good-humoured and sensible. In *Journey Without Maps* he says:

> Today our world seems peculiarly susceptible to
> brutality. There is a touch of nostalgia in the
> pleasure we take in gangster novels, in characters
> who have so agreeably simplified their emotions
> that they have begun living again at a level below
> the cerebral.

Crime-thrillers are nearer the primitive roots of Man—
in a way perhaps like mediaeval moralities or allegories
—and can show the comfortable, well-ordered surface
of life to be a vulnerable veneer. (William Golding, a
Catholic—Anglican not Roman—does something like
this in *Lord of the Flies*, using the conventions of the
adventure yarn about desert-island castaways.) Man
naturally lives and makes his decisions most of the
time at levels more profound than the cerebral. Thus
a literary form based on this belief (whether consciously
or not), which also presents a world in which treachery,
greed, vanity, violence and squalor predominate, is
nearer to fundamental realities than writing of a
tolerably liberal and progressive outlook which assumes
that through technological growth, reason and good-
humour the world is gradually becoming a better place.
Similarly, Greene was drawn to Africa and spent
several important periods of his life there and used
Africa significantly in his writings, because he felt that
more chances existed there of seeing life steadily and
seeing it whole than in a developed respectable
urbanized society. In the corrupt world of the gangster
and in the primitive jungle one is less likely to cherish
comforting illusions. Not, of course, that he advocates a
return to the primitive or a wish to stay there: 'but when

one sees to what peril of extinction centuries of
cerebration have brought us, one sometimes has a
curiosity to discover, if one can, from what we have
come, to recall at which point we went astray.' For
him in the jungle, as for J. M. Synge living among the
peasants of the west of Ireland, the basic issues were
plainer, less likely to be hidden, than they were in our
hectic, concrete and plastic, mechanized world. In
The Heart of the Matter, Scobie wonders why he is so
fond of Sierra Leone: 'Is it because here human nature
hasn't had time to disguise itself? Nobody here could
ever talk about a heaven on earth. Heaven remained
rigidly in its proper place on the other side of death,
and on this side flourished the injustices, the cruelties,
the meannesses, that elsewhere people so cleverly
hushed up. Here you could love human beings nearly
as God loved them, knowing the worst.' And in *The
Power and the Glory* the priest experiences something in
the close horror and confusion and stench of the
prison that makes the pious tea-parties and the sodalities
of his earlier years seem very unreal. The jungle hut,
then, is nearer reality than the semi-detached. And
the equivalent of the jungle in our society is the
underworld where the seedy, the despairing and the
polluted are more real than the chic, the complacent,
and the untouched, where Drewitt is more real than
one of J. B. Priestley's good companions. Thus, in
Brighton Rock, Brighton is a kind of jungle, reflecting
our beginnings, our lost innocence and our corruption,
yet not without grace.

This is marked from the beginning. Hale moves as
if in 'a thick forest in which a native could arrange his
poisoned ambush' and Pinkie is like a hunter 'before

the kill'. It is Pinkie's territory: 'the populous foreshore, a few thousand acres of house, a narrow peninsula of electrified track running to London, two or three railway stations with their buffets and buns'. (5, i). Kite had left him this inheritance which 'it was his duty never to leave for strange acres'.

It is worse than a natural jungle since it includes not only the original evil, atavistic fears and horrors, but also the evil of a corrupt, urban society, seedy and meretricious. Evil in some form or other, slight or enormous, alluring, ugly or furtive, is inescapable, from the gross luxuries and treacheries of the Cosmopolitan to the smelly dereliction of Nelson Place, from the tortured despair of Drewitt's house by the clanging rail-yard to the contemporary junk and scrub of the ill-made suburbs. Through intention or error, through the arrogance of the powerful or the carelessness of the mediocre, there is always pain and squalor and deception: Annie Collins, her head on the line waiting for the seven-five; the shambling blind men and Billy cuckolded; the car-park attendant whose every move is distressing; the rank Californian Poppy, the smell of cabbages and cooking and burnt cloth, the vulgarity of the newsagent's window, the dog's ordure on shoes at the wedding, the poisoned atmosphere of the fun-fair, and the discreditable secrets everyone has (known only to your mirror or bed-sheets), the weapon caressed or the tin of fruit drops hidden behind the book. Love-making, inevitably, is 'habitual, brutish and short', in the 'new raw street a couple pressed against each other', and Dallow and Judy kissing 'fought mouth to mouth . . . lips glued together in an attitude of angry passion: they might have been

inflicting on each other the greatest injury of which
either was capable.' (7, i).

The peculiar and memorable flavour of Brighton and
its inhabitants comes most of all from the pervasive
imagery of the novel. There are images of disease:
music bites like an abscess; sex is a sickness and marriage like velvet on a sore hand; Drewitt has an ulcer,
Pinkie an intermittent fever and Hale and Spicer have
a variety of disorders. There are especially unpleasant
images of mouths: Pinkie's mouth is stained purple;
Ida bestows her reward—'a soft gluey mouth affixed
in taxis'; the green tide sucks and slides 'like a wet
mouth round the piles'; 'the huge darkness presses a
wet mouth against the panes'; the broadcast cinema
organ drones 'across the crumby stained desert of
used cloths: the world's wet mouth lamenting over
life'; and Judy's mouth 'fastens, wet and prehensile,
like a sea-anemone', on a cheek. There are also
eruptions and pimples round her mouth and round
Spicer's. The associations between disease and violence
and sex are also connected with the images of war,
which are many and various. In addition to those
related to Ida (implacable 'like the wall at the end
of an alley scrawled with the obscene chalk messages of
an enemy') (7, i), there are simple ones such as the tide
'pounding at the piles like a boxer's fist against a
punchball in training for the human jaw', and Drewitt,
frightened, his face 'boarded up like a store when a
riot is on', and there are some in which several elements
coalesce, as in the 'dusty bunch of paper poppies, the
relic of an old November' in Judy's dressing gown as
she clinches with Dallow, in Pinkie's fixing the revolver
for Rose's suicide while the music wails upwards 'like

a dog over a grave', and in the marking of the essential difference between an abstract notion and a real experience—Pinkie knew the traditional actions of love, 'the game', in theory 'as a man may know the principles of gunnery in chalk on a blackboard, but to translate the knowledge to action, to the smashed village and the ravaged woman, one needed help from the nerves. His own were frozen with repulsion: to be touched, to give oneself away, to lay oneself open—he had held intimacy back as long as he could at the end of a razor blade.' (5, i).

Most frequent and dominating is the animal imagery. It occurs in names—Kite, Crab and Old Crowe, and even in objects, such as the Board which looks 'like something that has crept out of a drawer in a basement kitchen—a beetle'. Most of the animals are unattractive —small, slimy and fierce—and live close to the ground or under it—appropriately for a novel about the underworld. Tate sits 'like a large toad', Ida is like a ferret, Pinkie's hand is like a cold paddock, Judy's dead-white leg is 'like something which has lived underground', Drewitt's neighbours move like rats, his wife is like a mole, and giving him money is 'like fastening a leech onto the flesh'. Yet Drewitt depends on the large ranging life of the law, a lion, and he fears it, like a man who keeps 'a tame lion cub in his house' and can 'never be quite certain that the lion to whom he has taught so many tricks, to beg and eat out of his hand, might not one day unexpectedly mature and turn on him'. (7, iii). Also suitably, the shambling Dallow grins 'like a large and friendly dog' and 'his broad brutal and innocent face bears good news like a boar's head at a feast'. Rose also is associated with a mole, but in a different sense from Drewitt's wife. Rose reinforces the point (indicated on pages (19) and (80) here) that in her hole, in the jungle, there are enduring truths which are ignored in the slick and garish, smug and fun-seeking world outside.

There are also bird images. These, again very appropriately, embody another dimension and values. Apart from Old Crowe who is linked with superstition, and an owl 'on furry and predatory wings', crying 'with painful hunger swooping low over' Pinkie and suggesting hateful marriage (5, ii), the birds are gulls. Very significantly, gulls fly under the pier on two occasions. The first is when Spicer, so frightened that he doesn't notice the fatal photograph being taken, walks under the pier: 'A seagull flew straight towards him, between the pillars like a scared bird caught in a cathedral, then swerved out into the sunlight from the dark iron nave'. (3, ii). The second occurs when Pinkie returning from the inquest on Spicer is worrying about marriage: 'An old man went stooping down the shore, very slowly, turning the stones, picking among the dry seaweed for cigarette ends, scraps of food. The gulls which had stood like candles down the beach rose and cried under the promenade. The old man found a boot and stowed it in his sack, and a gull dropped from the parade and swept through the iron nave of the Palace Pier, white and purposeful in the obscurity: half vulture and half dove.' (5, i). The images are complex but something like the following appears there. The pier represents something uniquely precious —human life (which Spicer and Pinkie have destroyed) and also the Church, the agent of everlasting life and the only structure (iron pillars and nave) strong enough to withstand the stresses of the world. The gull represents the soul. Spicer is scared and caught by his crime but ignores the Church's warning. In relation to Pinkie, brought up as a Catholic, the image is more explicit: the gulls are like candles (prayers) and the flight of the bird recalls the beginning of Christianity in Britain. According to the Venerable Bede, King Edwin hears that the life of man is like the swift flight of a sparrow through a room. Greene in *Journey Without Maps* speaks of 'a story about a bird flying through a lighted hall playing its part in the conversion of a king', and there is a similar passage in *King Solomon's Mines*, which Greene knew: 'Like a storm-driven bird at night we fly out of Nowhere; for a moment our wings are seen in the light of the fire, and, lo, we are gone again into the Nowhere. Life is nothing. Life is all.' The flight of man should be white and purposeful (as Christ's was) but in us there is the unceasing war of our dual nature— half vulture and half dove—though we may be helped if our flight, our life, is, in essentials, in and through the Church. Pinkie rejects this and goes on to seek vainly practice with Sylvie for his 'game' of mortal sin with Rose.

There is a further point. Under the pier Spicer stumbles on 'an old boot' and puts 'his hand on the stones to save himself'. But he does not save himself spiritually. Later the old man stows the boot in his sack. Spicer has missed his chance. This old man is mysterious. He appears on two more occasions, before and after Ida's 'bit of fun' with Corkery. He is always stooping and searching, and he disinters with infinite patience 'some relic from the shingle'. (5, vi). He may represent some spiritual force constantly operating, a humble and shaded reflection, perhaps, of Keats's magnificent:

'moving waters at their priest-like task
Of pure ablution round earth's human shores'.

There are related implications in the other bird images. They show goodness and grace trying to get through to Pinkie. Rose wishes to unite herself completely with Pinkie, but he resists: 'her words scratched tentatively at the barrier like a bird's claws on the window pane: he could feel her all the time trying to get at him; even her humility seemed a trap.' (6, ii). And as Pinkie drives to damnation, the Holy Ghost, traditionally a bird, makes a supreme effort to save him: 'An enormous emotion beat on him; it was like something trying to get in, the pressure of gigantic wings against the glass.' (7, ix).

Pinkie withstands it. He refuses to let it move him to demolish the hideous fabric built up during his seventeen years, to let redemption operate. He will not serve and be freed. He remains true to his setting. As he claims, 'with dreary pride', he is the 'real Brighton—as if his single heart contained all the cheap amusements, the Pullman cars, the unloving weekends at the gaudy hotels'. And Brighton, as Drewitt declares, and as almost everything that happens demonstrates, is Hell, or rather is very near to Hell. And it is a microcosm. This is decisively implied by the various allusions and echoes—historical, literary, social and metaphysical—and confirmed by all the newspaper reports: 'Violet Crowe violated and buried under the West Pier, . . . Scene at Council Meeting . . . Collision in Clarence Street, . . . Assault on Schoolgirl in Epping

Forest'. The contagion of the savage, reeking pit is inescapable. No one is innocent. This is a cursed and fallen world. But incontrovertible as all this is, it is not quite the whole story. Rose and Piker and the birds are there also, and there is the pier attached to the land yet related to other elements.

Questions

1. Analyse the two major confrontations between Rose and Ida.

2. Write a conversation between Ida, Sylvie and Judy in which they talk about and compare and sum-up their men.

3. Write a report from Crab to Colleoni immediately after the carving of Brewer about Pinkie's gang, describing its background, size, strength, weakness, the natures of its members and how it might be dealt with. Describe Colleoni's reaction to this assessment and his decision.

4. Consider the ways in which Greene gives individuality to his minor characters.

5. Write a conversation between Rose and Piker about Pinkie six months after his death.

6. In what ways is *Brighton Rock* a 'social document' of its period and setting and how far is it relevant today?

7. Compared to any nineteenth-century novels you know, in what sense is *Brighton Rock* modern in techniques of characterization and narration?

STYLE, INVOLVEMENT and ACHIEVEMENT

Greene's style is sinewy and spare, producing very economically a diversity of apt effects. He avoids the abstract and the general and keeps close to recognizable facts and presents them in such a way as to suggest wider and more enduring meanings; the brisk impact of the singularly vivid instance sets up resonances which go far beyond it. His rhythms are drawn from everyday speech and he rarely attempts any strongly marked or extended rhythmical or rhetorical effects—the sound properly echoes and does not overbear the sense. His strength comes mainly from his conciseness, his imagery, his juxtapositions and allusions, his comparisons and contrasts, his irony, and the remarkable adroitness of his links and transitions between sentences, between paragraphs and between chapters. Examples of all these appeared earlier in the course of discussion of construction, narrative, character and so on. This is inevitable, as style is not something that can be considered in the abstract; it cannot be separated from content. Style is not something elegant or striking stuck on to the matter but is an essential part of it. Style is those words (and those alone) in that order (and that alone), the best and seemingly inevitable and only way of presenting something.

Nevertheless, the style of an important writer is always distinctive no matter what he is dealing with. The style is very much the man. This is true of Greene. There is a flavour about his writing which can always be recognized even if it cannot be defined. And he not only gives life to a character, incident or scene but he also powerfully suggests an attitude. Take the account of Hale's funeral. In 'a bare cold secular chapel which could be adapted quietly and conveniently to any creed' the anonymous clergyman rolls out in a 'cultured, inexpressive heartless voice' the woolliest waffle, stamping 'his words, like little pats of butter, with his personal mark', then he presses a buzzer to launch Hale in his coffin through the New Art doors down the slipway into the furnace, and smiles gently 'like a conjurer who has produced his nine hundred and fortieth rabbit without a hitch'. From the stately brick towers fumes 'the very last of Fred, a thin stream of grey smoke from the ovens. People passing up the flowery suburban road looked up and noted the smoke; it had been a busy day at the furnaces. Fred dropped in indistinguishable grey ash on the pink blossoms: he became part of the smoke nuisance over London, and Ida wept.' (i, iii). Greene's prejudices stick out a mile, but this is still brilliant, black satiric comedy at its most scathing. The scene is not essential for the action of the novel, but it is for its theme. The scene, together with the marriage in the disinfected municipal building, shows Greene's fastidious loathing of puritanism, his intense dislike of attempts to smooth over or soar above the mystery, the squalor, the pain which are part of the horror and glory of being alive. Fred's 'bright new flowery suburb' is more hygienic than Nelson Place but the people who are at ease there are less potent for good or evil than Rose and her parents. The scene is part of Greene's basic position that Pinkie is more human than Colleoni, that the derelict old woman is more human than Ida. A classic statement of this view occurs in T. S. Eliot's essay on Baudelaire:

So far as we are human, what we do must be either evil or good; so far as we do evil or good we are human; and it is better, in a paradoxical way, to do evil than to do nothing: at least, we exist. It is true to say that the glory of man is his capacity for salvation; it is also true to say that his glory is his capacity for damnation. The worst that can be said of most of our malefactors, from statesmen to thieves, is that they are not men enough to be damned.

The big danger of this view is that it may be used to uphold an unjust social order and to block attempts to do away with slums and to help people towards better living conditions. This danger is avoided by Greene, however. He makes it clear that Pinkie's environment is largely responsible for what he is. Because he has never known love he fails to respond to Rose, and when God is trying so hard to get to him it is the hideous forces shaping Pinkie from birth that bitterly resist. In this Greene is one with his liberal contemporaries who affirm that psychological and environmental factors are mainly to blame for human corruption and suffering and that if we improve these factors people will probably have better lives. Greene, though, denies that this explains everything. For him, the heart of the matter is man's fallen condition, his predilection for evil which theologians call original sin. An essence of this belief occurs memorably in Newman's *Apologia Pro Vita Sua*, part of which is quoted as one of the epigraphs to Greene's *The Lawless Roads*: 'either there is no Creator, or this living society of men is in a true sense discarded from His presence . . . *if* there be a God, *since* there is a God, the human race is implicated in some terrible aboriginal calamity.' Therefore the progressive humanist view that denies the reality of evil and seeks to process away sin through mental guidance and social engineering (helpful though these may be) is quite inadequate. Greene arrived at this position early in life and long before he became a Catholic.

He was driven to it by the unhappiness of his childhood and through his reading, as he makes clear in *The Lost Childhood*. It was the reading at the age of fourteen of Marjorie Bowen's *The Viper of Milan* that was crucial: then his 'future for better or worse really struck'. This book explained his 'terrible living world', the unwholesomeness, the furtive fears and treacheries, the superior attractiveness and reality of failure over success. Characters such as Visconti, 'with his beauty, his patience and his genius for evil', Greene recognized in his own life: 'I had watched him pass by many a time in his black Sunday suit smelling of mothballs . . . He exercised terror from a distance like a snowcloud over the young fields. Goodness has only once found a perfect incarnation in a human body and never will again, but evil can always find a home there. Human nature is not black and white but black and grey. I read all that in *The Viper of Milan* and I looked round and I saw that it was so . . . Miss Bowen had given me my pattern—religion might later explain it to me in other terms, but the pattern was already there—perfect evil walking the world where perfect good can never walk again, and only the pendulum ensures that after all in the end justice is done.' For Greene as for Pinkie the shape and texture of life was set in youth as it was for mankind in its youth in the Garden. Greene's quotation from A. E.'s poem 'Germinal' is completely apt:

> In ancient shadows and twilights
>   Where childhood had strayed,
> The world's great sorrows were born
>   And its heroes were made.
> In the lost boyhood of Judas
>   Christ was betrayed.

Hence the emphasis on the significance of childhood, the indelible nature of early experience, of the loss of innocence, in *Brighton Rock*. Yet there remains an area, sometimes, as in Pinkie's case, very slight, for free will. Man has a choice. Though his horrible upbringing may have stunted and perverted him, though his innate bias towards evil may be strong, he can, through the grace of God, achieve goodness. All is not determined by material factors; the slums produce Roses and Pikers as well as Pinkies where the Church is fulfilling its mission.

All this is apparent in *Brighton Rock*. It presents a fallen world, a polluted jungle where cruelty and squalor and pride predominate. The world of right and wrong, Colleoni and Ida and their followers, thrive, and evil is at home and busy, while good seems hardly to stir. The pervasive atmosphere of ugliness and destruction has led some people to conclude that Greene loathes everyday existence and regards the world as given over to the Devil. But this is not so. Apart from the saving gleams of wit and humour and the vivacity of his sense impressions of the world (an obsessive hatred would not produce such apt accuracy) there is a realistic concern which makes him ironical (something of Swift's savage indignation beneath the urbanity) and so determined to expose the hollowness of false or flattering beliefs and to indicate valid ones no matter how daunting they may appear.

Wrong and evil seem supreme in Brighton and in the world (both of which seem synonymous with Hell), and Brighton, the world, seems to belong to the Evil One. But, in fact, it is illegally occupied by him, not completely ruled or owned, and bands owing allegiance to its Creator fight on, and there 'lives the dearest freshness deep down things'. Pinkie may stalk, a Satanic figure, his will to do evil, if not his means, as great almost as the Devil's, and perfect goodness is not present in human form; but the effect of the one Incarnation, 'a full, perfect and sufficient sacrifice . . .', the grace abounding that it provides, is such that the humble Rose is elevated into something like sainthood. Hence even the worst can be overcome. Rose has an intimation of this as she drives with Pinkie towards the end. He shrinks from her and she has an awful doubt: 'if this was the darkest nightmare of all, if he didn't love her'. But she is able to accept even this: 'It didn't matter; she loved him'. (7, vii). This simply is the nucleus of the novel, its fundamental affirmation. She loved him, and nothing else really mattered, as 'God so loved the world that he gave his only begotten Son . . .' She loves him, and so she can face the worst horror of all at the end. God loves us and so we can face our various horrors in our jungles and Brightons.

Those of us who are Christians, that is. And for those who are not there is a vicarious experience of Christianity through the novel. Our disbelief is willingly suspended and we are led to understand and to feel upon our pulses values and attitudes that we might be indifferent to in any other form. There is that release from routine preoccupations and that identification with persons and ways other than our own, that widening and deepening of human sympathies which come from a work of imagination, imagination which is, in Shelley's words, 'the great instrument of moral good'. This then is the achievement of *Brighton Rock*, that it endows and combines, meeting several needs and operating on several levels, each supporting and blending with the others—the crime-thriller, the sociological tale and the religious novel.

Questions

1. Illustrate and discuss Greene's use of detail in *Brighton Rock*.

2. Pick out any instances of humour and indicate their function.

3. How far is it true to say that Greene has a low opinion of the mass of mankind?

4. What, if anything, would a person who saw a film of *Brighton Rock* without reading the novel miss?

5. Read Marjorie Bowen's *The Viper of Milan* and specify what bearing it seems to have on *Brighton Rock*.

6. What considerations would you bear in mind in assessing a novel?

FURTHER READING

Allen, Walter, 'Awareness of Evil: Graham Greene', in *Nation*, CLXXXII (21 April 1956), 344–46.

Allott, Kenneth, and Miriam Farris, *The Art of Graham Greene*, London, Hamish Hamilton, 1951, reprinted New York, Russell & Russell, 1963.

Evans, Robert O., ed., *Graham Greene:* some critical considerations, University of Kentucky Press, 1963.

Kermode, Frank, 'Mr. Greene's Eggs and Crosses' in *Puzzles and Epiphanies*, London, Routledge & Kegan Paul, 1962, 176–87.

Kunkel, Francis L., *The Labyrinthine Ways of Graham Greene*, New York, Sheed & Ward, 1960.

Lees, F. N., 'Graham Greene: a Comment', in *Scrutiny*, XIX (1952), 31–42.

Modern Fiction Studies, Graham Greene Special Number, III, Autumn 1957.

O'Donnell, Donat (pseud. Conor Cruise O'Brien), 'Graham Greene: the Anatomy of Pity' in *Maria Cross*, New York, Oxford University Press, 1952, 63–94.

Pryce-Jones, David, *Graham Greene*, Edinburgh, Oliver & Boyd, 1963.

NOTES ON ENGLISH LITERATURE

Chief Adviser: JOHN D. JUMP, *Professor of English Literature in the University of Manchester*

General Editor: W. H. MASON, *Lately Senior English Master, The Manchester Grammar School*